Keep it professional, Parker.

Aimee sighed in her sleep, and half turned, so that her cheek was no more than an inch from his nose. He could see the faint dusting of freckles on her smooth skin. The scent of lemon and the delicate curve of her cheek made his mouth water.

He breathed deeply and tried to relax. For the moment, they were safe. He needed to get as much rest as he could while he had the chance. Because tomorrow wasn't going to be easy. Tomorrow, he was going to have to explain to her why they were pressed up against each other and practically naked.

And why he hadn't kept his promise to her—his promise to place her baby safely into her arms before the day was out.

MALLORY KANE

HIS BEST FRIEND'S BABY

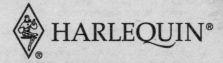

HARLEQUIN®

TORONTO • NEW YORK • LONDON
AMSTERDAM • PARIS • SYDNEY • HAMBURG
STOCKHOLM • ATHENS • TOKYO • MILAN • MADRID
PRAGUE • WARSAW • BUDAPEST • AUCKLAND

For Michael, for the usual reasons.

Recycling programs
for this product may
not exist in your area.

ISBN-13: 978-0-373-69425-9

HIS BEST FRIEND'S BABY

Copyright © 2009 by Rickey R. Mallory

This edition published by arrangement with Harlequin Books S.A.

® and TM are trademarks of the publisher. Trademarks indicated with ® are registered in the United States Patent and Trademark Office, the Canadian Trade Marks Office and in other countries.

www.eHarlequin.com

Printed in U.S.A.

ABOUT THE AUTHOR

Mallory Kane credits her love of books to her mother, a librarian, who taught her that books are a precious resource and should be treated with loving respect. Her father and grandfather were steeped in the Southern tradition of oral history, and could hold an audience spellbound for hours with their storytelling skills. Mallory aspires to be as good a storyteller as her father.

Mallory lives in Mississippi with her computer-genius husband, their two fascinating cats and, at current count, seven computers. She loves to hear from readers. You can write her at mallory@mallorykane.com or via Harlequin Books.

Books by Mallory Kane

CAST OF CHARACTERS

Matt Parker—When Aimee's baby is kidnapped, Matt vows to risk anything, even his life, to save the son of his best friend's widow. Will he ever be able to do right by the woman he loves?

Aimee Vick—She holds Matt responsible for her husband's death, but when her precious child is kidnapped, there's no one she trusts more to bring her child back to her safe and sound. But trusting him with her heart is another matter entirely.

Deke Cunningham—He's not exactly a poster child for responsibility. Can Matt depend on him when the chips are down?

Margo Vick—Aimee Vick's mother-in-law wants control of her grandson so she can control the Vick Hotel fortune. Would she endanger the baby's life to prove Aimee an unfit mother?

Aaron Gold—Aaron is a computer whiz whose father died on a mission under Rook Castle's command. Does he blame Rook for depriving him of a father?

Brock O'Neill—A former navy SEAL who lost an eye while in the service, he's terse and secretive. No one really knows who he is or where he goes when he disappears.

Rafiq Jackson—Rafiq was born in England of a Muslim mother and British father. He speaks several languages and is a mathematical genius who worked for the NSA. But where do his loyalties lie?

Prologue

The cold rain beat down on the white roses that blanketed Bill Vick's coffin, turning them yellow and soggy. The canopy flapped and creaked in the wind.

A dozen or so people had braved the weather to attend the graveside service, but Matthew Parker saw only one—Aimee Vick, his best friend's widow.

From his vantage point, several dozen feet away and partially hidden by trees, Matt could barely see the strands of brown hair that had escaped from beneath her hat to blow across her pale face.

Aimee didn't notice. She stood stiffly, her arms folded protectively across her tummy, nodding and smiling sadly as people filed by, offering their condolences one more time before they headed home.

Matt pushed his fists deeper into his pockets and hunched his shoulders against the bone-deep chill that shuddered through him. A chill that had nothing to do with the cold April wind or the freezing rain that poured off the brim of his Stetson.

Three days before, he'd done the two most difficult things he'd ever done in his life. He'd brought Bill's body home to Sundance, Wyoming, and he'd faced Bill's wife and tried to explain how a weekend adventure had turned into tragedy.

How, in the blink of an eye, she was widowed, and her unborn baby would never know his father.

Her utter shock and disbelief had been agonizing to watch, but he'd stood there, needing to see it. Just as he did now. He needed to share her grief, her pain.

Aimee wiped her cheek with a gloved finger, and bowed her head for an instant.

Matt's eyes stung. He blinked and looked at his watch. He needed to leave now. His flight back to the tiny border province of Mahjidastan was scheduled to leave in an hour.

For a few seconds, he debated whether he should speak to her. But he quelled the notion as soon as it surfaced. Seeing him would only hurt her more.

He'd known Aimee nearly as long as he'd known Bill, which was most of his life. He'd kidded Bill about not deserving her. She was generous and kind, and forgiving to a fault. She gave everyone the benefit of the doubt, until they proved they didn't deserve it.

Three days ago, Matt had proven he didn't deserve her forgiveness. She hadn't said it, but the look in her eyes had spoken louder than words.

If not for him, Bill would still be alive. He'd be safe at home with his wife, awaiting the birth of their son.

Bill's death was his fault.

Chapter One

A year later
THURSDAY 0900 HOURS

Matt Parker stepped outside Irina Castle's ranch house, the headquarters for Black Hills Search and Rescue in Sundance, Wyoming, and headed for the helipad a few hundred yards to the east. He lifted his head and took a deep breath of crisp, fresh Wyoming air.

The day before, for the first time in a year, he'd set foot on American soil, on Wyoming soil. He was back home, where he belonged. He loved the Black Hills. Even though they'd tried to kill him and his three best friends twenty years ago, he loved them. They sustained him.

He'd done his best to track down any rumors of Americans in the remote mountain province of Mahjidastan, which was located in a disputed border area shared by Afghanistan, Pakistan and China. His objective had been to find Rook Castle, Irina's husband. But ultimately, he'd failed, as had BHSAR specialist Aaron Gold before him. And now Irina had called off the search.

As he circled the Bell 429 helicopter that was BHSAR Specialist Deke Cunningham's baby, another fellow specialist, Brock O'Neill, appeared in the doorway of the hangar.

"Parker," he said as Matt approached. The terse greeting was typical of the ex-Navy SEAL. He held out his hand and cocked his head—the only indication Matt had ever seen that the patch over his left eye bothered him.

Matt shook his hand. "Brock. How're you doing?"

"Hmph. Watch out. Your buddy's in a mood." Brock broke the handshake and headed toward the ranch house.

Matt suppressed a smile as he continued toward the hangar. For Brock, that was a warm greeting.

When he stepped through the open door, Deke was leaning back in his desk chair with his feet propped up, tossing a steel bearing from hand to hand. A small TV was tuned to a morning news show, its sound muted.

"Hey, Deke," Matt said. "Playing catch with yourself?"

Deke's feet hit the floor and he set the silver ball on his desk. "That goober I just hired overtightened a bolt and ruined this ball bearing. Brock offered to take him out for me."

Matt laughed.

"How're you doing?"

Matt took Deke's hand. "Been a while. Can't say I'm glad to see you."

"I know."

"Man, I hate this," Matt said, nodding back toward the ranch house. "The place feels like a funeral home. I didn't see Irina. How's she holding up?"

Deke shook his head. "She's trying to act like she's fine, but she's not. She's in bad shape." Deke wiped a hand over his face and then pushed his shaggy hair back. "She's in town this morning, talking to her accountant again."

"So it's true?" Matt asked. "All her funds are wiped out?"

Deke nodded. "All her personal funds. Damn Rook for not signing everything over to her when they got married. I'd like to kill him—" Deke stopped and clamped his jaw.

Matt snorted. "Too late. But it's not like he knew he was going to die."

"No?" Deke's brows lowered and his blue eyes turned black. "He spent his whole life stepping in front of bullets for other people. He had to figure one would hit him sooner or later."

"I don't get it. She's his wife—widow. Why doesn't she get his money?"

"It's all about the suspicious nature of his death. Just because they don't have a body—greedy bastards."

"Hang on a minute," Matt said as he glanced at the TV. "Turn that up."

Deke scooped up the remote control and tossed it to him. "What is it?"

"Check out the pink dress. It's Margo Vick."

"Bill's mother? Opening another Vick Resort Hotel?"

"Not this time. That's FBI Special Agent Aaron Schiff standing next to her." Matt hit the volume control.

"—I am personally offering a reward for any information leading to the kidnapper."

Kidnapper. Alarm pierced Matt's chest as Margo

yielded the microphone to the FBI special agent. Among the dark suits, her brightly colored dress drew all eyes to her.

"We plan to hold press conferences on a regular basis, and we'll update the media as we have more information," Special Agent Schiff said. "Meanwhile, please let us do our job. Our primary concern is getting Mrs. Vick's grandson back home safe and sound."

"It's Aimee's baby. He's been kidnapped." Matt sat on the edge of a folding chair and propped his elbows on his knees, listening as Schiff answered questions from reporters. The cameras pulled back to reveal the front of the Vick mansion, located just outside Casper, Wyoming. Besides Schiff and Margo, several uniformed police officers stood on the marble steps, along with a couple of men in suits.

Matt's gaze zeroed in on a pale face behind Bill's mother. It was Aimee, dressed in something dark that blended with the suits and uniforms. Her eyes were huge and strands of hair blew across her face.

"There's Aimee." He didn't take his eyes off her until the camera switched back to Schiff. Then he shot up off the chair and paced, rubbing his thumb across his lower lip.

"There's something more going on here," he said as dread pressed on his chest like a weight.

"What—with the kidnapping?"

"About a month ago, my journal disappeared from my room."

Deke frowned and picked up the ball bearing again. He tossed it back and forth. "You mean on your laptop?"

Matt shook his head. With every passing second,

pressure in his chest grew. "I keep notes in a small leather journal just for my use. I write my reports to Irina from my notes. You know, rumors of Americans in the area, anything I can glean about what Novus Ordo or his terrorist friends are up to, lists of expenses."

"You think it was stolen?"

He nodded.

"Okay. How does this have anything to do with the grandbaby of one of the wealthiest women in Wyoming being kidnapped?"

Matt glanced back at the TV, but there was a commercial on. "Work stuff wasn't all that was in the journal."

He turned toward the window, letting his gaze roam over the jagged peaks in the distance. "It's been a year since Bill died, and I haven't talked to her."

Deke didn't comment.

Matt rubbed his lip. "I just couldn't face her. So I was trying to compose a letter. A way to—tell her how sorry I am."

"I don't follow."

"Novus knows we've been searching for any clue that Rook survived his sniper attack. I've been followed ever since I got over there. I'm sure whoever stole my journal was sent by Novus, so now—"

"Now he knows how you feel about Aimee," Deke supplied. He set the ball bearing down and sat up straight.

"How I feel—?" Matt frowned. "Well, yeah. He knows about her baby and about me being William's godfather. And now Irina's stopped looking for Rook. What if Novus thinks she stopped because I found him?"

"And what? You think Novus had Aimee's baby kidnapped—"

"To get to me."

Deke blew out a long breath. "Kind of a stretch. Why wouldn't he have grabbed you before now if he thought you knew something?"

"Think about it. I've been in Mahjidastan for the past year, searching for information about the only man on the earth who could identify Novus Ordo. And before me Aaron was there for a year. There hasn't been a day since Rook disappeared off that boat that a BHSAR specialist hasn't been looking for him. Suddenly, Irina pulls me out and doesn't replace me. Novus didn't have a chance to get his hands on me. I left within four hours of Irina's phone call."

Deke gave a short, sharp laugh. "That's quite a conspiracy theory. But it makes sense—sort of. What now?"

Matt met Deke's gaze and set his jaw. "If Novus Ordo has taken Aimee Vick's baby to try and get his hands on me to interrogate me about Rook, I'm going to make it easy for him."

So far everything was working well. Not bad for a plan that had been put together in less than twenty-four hours.

The Vick baby was already in safe hands. The FBI was on the case. And, most important, Parker was acting exactly as predicted. He was inserting himself right into the middle of the kidnapping investigation.

A warm sense of satisfaction spread through him. It was immaterial whether Rook Castle was alive or dead. He had a larger goal. And finally, it was in sight.

He looked at his watch. Almost time. He had a telephone call to make.

THURSDAY 1430 HOURS

AIMEE VICK PACED back and forth across the living room of her mother-in-law's house. The room was crawling with FBI special agents, uniformed police officers, and technicians trailing spools of wire everywhere.

She looked at the grandfather clock for the hundredth time—or the thousandth. Two-thirty p.m. It had been eight hours. Eight miserable, terrifying hours without her baby.

When she'd woken up this morning and discovered that William was gone, she'd have sworn she couldn't survive eight hours without her baby. But she was still alive, and still rational—barely.

William Matthew was only seven months old, and she'd never spent a night without him. Hardly even an hour. He was her anchor, her life since her husband's death.

She didn't notice that someone else had come in the front door until she heard her name called.

She turned and found herself face-to-face with Matt Parker, her husband's best friend, her baby's godfather, and the last man on earth she expected to see.

"Matt," she croaked. Her voice was hoarse and sounded harsh to her ears.

The last time she'd seen him was a year ago, when he'd brought her husband's body home. He looked just as stricken as he had that day.

Her first impulse was to run to him and hug him. But she didn't. Her emotions were already in turmoil, and seeing Matt made things even more confusing.

She should be furious at him. After all, he hadn't shown up for Bill's funeral, nor for William Matthew's christening, even though she'd honored Bill's request to name him as William's godfather.

She'd spent a good portion of the past year filled with anger. At Matt for taking Bill skydiving. At Bill for going off and dying. At herself for not putting her foot down and refusing to let him go.

Matt looked down and rubbed the back of his neck. After a few seconds, he raised his head enough to meet her gaze. "Aimee, I'm so sorry about your baby. I've talked with Special Agent Schiff. He's agreed to let me help with the investigation—if you'll agree."

Aimee clutched at her abdomen, where the hollow nausea that had been her constant companion ever since Bill died was growing, threatening to cut off her breath.

"How did you get here?" She shook her head. "I mean, it just happened this morning—".

"It doesn't matter. I'm here. Will you let me help?"

Aimee looked at Special Agent Schiff, who nodded at her reassuringly. "I can't believe—I haven't seen you since—"

Matt's gaze faltered. "I know. I'm sorry, Aimee."

Aimee started when Margo laid a hand on her shoulder—a heavy hand. "Aimee, dear, why don't you get a glass of water?"

"Thank you, Margo, but I'm not thirsty." She tried to step away from her mother-in-law's grasp, but Margo held on.

"I'd like to speak to Matthew alone for a moment."

Aimee rubbed her temple, where a headache was gathering. She knew what Margo planned to do. She was going to tell Matt to leave. She could practically see the wheels turning in her mother-in-law's head. A lot of people in Casper knew that Matt had been with Bill when he died, and Margo didn't like the Vicks being the subject of gossip.

Appearances. They'd always been her main concern. The magenta suit she wore attested to that. Only Aimee and the owner of Margo's favorite dress shop knew that her first act upon hearing of her grandson's kidnapping was to have the suit rushed over in time for the press conference.

"Anything you have to say, you can say in front of me, Margo." Aimee stiffened her back and met her mother-in-law's gaze.

"If you're sure, dear." Margo turned to Matt. "Aimee is terribly distraught. I'd rather she not be upset further. Perhaps you should leave."

Matt raised his brows and gazed at Margo steadily. "I have every right to be here. William Matthew is my godson."

A godson he'd never seen, Aimee thought. To make matters worse, Margo had spent the year since Bill's death trying to coax Aimee to relinquish control of William's future to her.

I have the resources and the connections, dear. You don't.

Grief and fear and anger balled up inside Aimee, until she felt as if she were going to explode. She had to bite her tongue to keep from lashing out at both of them.

Aimee had loved Bill, but the six years of their marriage had been a tug-of-war between him and his mother. Now she was in the same position, standing between Margo and Matt.

"William is my child," she blurted out. "This is my decision."

Every eye in the room turned their way.

"Aimee," Margo said warningly as her fingers tightened on Aimee's shoulder. "Don't make a scene."

Aimee wasn't sure how she felt about Matt showing up after a year—almost to the day—since Bill's death, but she didn't doubt his ability. As a weather expert and survival specialist, rescuing the innocent was his specialty.

If anyone could save her child, Matt could.

"If Special Agent Schiff agrees, I want Matt here. It makes sense for him to be involved. He's trained in rescue and recov—" Aimee's throat closed on the word *recovery*.

"Rescue," she said as firmly as she could. *No crying.* She hadn't cried yet, and she didn't plan to start now. Crying never helped anything. She was afraid that if she started she wouldn't be able to stop.

Margo's dark eyes snapped with irritation as she drew in a sharp breath. Then, with a quick glance around the room, she consciously relaxed her face and nodded.

"Of course," she said stiffly. "I didn't mean to imply otherwise." Her grip on Aimee's shoulder loosened and turned into an awkward pat.

The shrill ring of a cell phone split the air. Aimee jumped.

It was him. The kidnapper.

She whirled, looking for her purse, and then remembered that the FBI had forwarded her cell to Margo's house phone. At that instant, the landline rang.

Special Agent Schiff motioned her over to the table, where wires and headphones and computers appeared to be piled haphazardly.

"Mrs. Vick—" Schiff said in a cautionary tone. "Remember what we discussed?"

She was going to have to talk to the man who'd taken her baby. Her stomach turned upside down. As she approached, a computer technician handed two sets of headphones to Schiff. Schiff, in turn, reached past her to hand a set to Matt. Then he donned the remaining set himself.

"Wait to see what he says," Schiff cautioned her. "Once he starts talking ransom, you insist it be delivered by a family friend—Parker. Don't let him bully you. Don't give in to any demands. *You* are in control, not him. Got it?"

Aimee had never felt less in control in her life. Her baby was in the hands of the monster on the other end of the phone, and she was being forced to bargain for his life. The phone rang again, the piercing noise sending terror slicing through her.

"On my count," Schiff whispered. "Pick up on three."

She nodded jerkily. Her throat was too dry to swallow. Her hands were shaking so much she wasn't sure she could hold on to the phone.

Schiff nodded at the computer tech, glanced at Matt, then held up a finger. "One," he mouthed to her.

A second finger went up. "Two."

Aimee bit her lip and reached for the phone. Matt stepped closer.

Schiff held up three fingers. "Three." He nodded.

She picked up the phone, her other hand pressed to her chest. "Hello?" she croaked.

"Hello, Aimee. Hello, Special Agent Schiff, and whoever else is listening."

Aimee stiffened at the kidnapper's menacing tone. At the same time, Matt's shoulder brushed hers. Coiled tension radiated from his body like heat. He rested a hand lightly on the small of her back. Somehow, his touch gave her courage.

"What have you done with my baby?" she cried. "I have to know if he's okay."

"Your baby is perfectly safe for now," the harsh voice said. "It's up to you to keep him safe. Let's talk business."

"What do you want?" she asked tightly.

"Money, of course," the man replied. "Are you listening, Schiff? Because I will only say this once. I want a million dollars in hundreds. Don't give me any problem about the money. I am aware of who your mother-in-law is." The man's voice was cold and hard. "I don't want to hear excuses about needing time to get the cash together. Just do it."

Aimee felt helpless and lost. She could hardly make sense of what he was saying. She took a deep breath. "Let me talk to my baby," she begged. "He must be so scared. He needs to hear my voice."

"Shut up. You're not giving the orders. I am. Now here's where the exchange will take place."

He rattled off some numbers that meant nothing to Aimee. Out of the corner of her eye, she saw Matt nod at Schiff.

"Got it?" the man snapped.

Schiff sent her a nod.

"Y-yes," she said.

"Tomorrow at 1500 hours. Aimee, if you want to see your baby again, *you* will deliver the money."

Matt jerked. He shook his head fiercely at Schiff.

"I—I don't know," she stammered, her heart stuck in her throat.

"Family friend," Schiff mouthed.

"Wait. I can't come alone," she said as strongly as she could. "I—I'll need to care for William Matthew. I need to bring a—a family friend—"

"Schiff?" the kidnapper said. "What did I tell you? I will not say it again. Make it happen."

The line went dead.

"Dammit," Matt spat.

Aimee's throat closed and her eyes stung with tears. She swallowed them as the phone dropped from her numb fingers. "What is it? What's wrong?" she asked.

Schiff didn't answer her. "Give me those coordinates," he told the computer tech, who repeated the numbers.

"You said you're an expert in weather and survival," Schiff said to Matt. "Know where that is?"

"That latitude and longitude puts it north of Sundance," Matt muttered. He pulled a small device out of his pocket and pressed buttons. "It's about halfway up Ragged Top Mountain. Rough terrain. Plus we've got a late-winter storm building. Could dump a foot or more of snow before it's done."

He turned toward Margo. "Isn't Ragged Top where your husband's hunting cabin was? I think Bill and I went up there a few times."

Margo nodded stiffly. "That's right. No one's been

there in years. I don't understand. What did the kidnapper say?"

"He's demanding that we bring the money to a location on the south side of Ragged Top."

"South—? That's—" Margo stopped, frowning. "Oh, dear." Her face drained of color.

It was only the second time Aimee had ever seen Margo shaken. The first was when she was told her son had died. Maybe her mother-in-law wasn't as cold and insensitive as she'd always appeared.

"What?" Matt demanded. "It's what?"

The woman blinked. "Nothing. It's just—it's so hard to get up there. Especially this time of year. I'd have thought—I mean how's he going to keep William safe up there?"

"I'll tell you how," Matt said. "He knows the area. I'd bet money on it, judging by the way he rattled off those coordinates. He knows Aimee can't go by herself."

Schiff raised his eyebrows. "What about you? Can you do it?"

Matt's jaw clenched in determination. "Yeah. I can do it. I've pulled innocents out of more remote locations than that. But this storm's coming in fast. By 1500 hours tomorrow, it'll be right on top of that peak."

Schiff frowned. "The weather service said it would be moving into this area late tomorrow night."

"Yeah, that's what they're saying." Matt set his jaw. "I'm going in alone."

Aimee stiffened. She knew he could do it. That wasn't the problem. He was a search-and-rescue specialist, trained in the Air Force. There was no one better suited to the job.

But the kidnapper had been very specific.

"Don't even think about leaving me behind, Matt," she said. "William Matthew is my baby. He needs me. When you hand over the money, *I* will be there to take him in my arms."

Chapter Two

After coordinating times and plans with Special Agent Schiff, Matt drove straight back to Castle Ranch. He needed to talk to Deke.

At thirty, Deke Cunningham was one of the most decorated Air Force combat rescue officers alive. His skill with a rifle was legendary. The only thing he did better than shoot was fly a helicopter.

Which was exactly why Matt wanted him on alert for the ransom exchange.

When he got to the hangar, Deke wasn't there. But at the door to his office, Matt saw something he hadn't noticed before.

The plaque hanging beside Deke's office door. It had hung in Rook Castle's office since the day he'd created Black Hills Search and Rescue, Incorporated. It was small and plain, with a simple message.

IN MEMORIAM
Vietnam Veteran and Combat Rescue Officer

Arlis Hanks, 1944–1990. Our pledge—to honor
your bravery by rescuing the innocent.

Matt touched the four signatures that were embla-
zoned into the bronze. Robert Kenneth Castle, Deke
Cunningham, Matthew Parker and William Barker Vick.

Irina must have given it to Deke. Matt nodded to
himself. It was fitting.

He found Deke in Irina's office, sitting with her,
Specialist Rafiq Jackson and Aaron Gold near a bank
of windows that framed a view of the desolate, magnifi-
cent Black Hills. He nodded at Rafe and Aaron, and ac-
knowledged Deke with a brief glance.

Irina smiled and stood to give him a hug. Rook
Castle's widow was as vibrant and lovely as ever. Her
blond hair glowed in the sunlight that streamed in the
window. But behind her smile and the sparkle in her
blue eyes, Matt saw a shadow of grief.

He couldn't imagine how difficult it had been for her
to give up searching for her husband. She'd seen him
shot, and watched him fall into the Mediterranean Sea.
Even so, she'd clung to the hope that because his body
had never been recovered, he might be alive.

Now, she'd given up. For everyone who knew her,
and who'd supported her efforts to find him, that made
it official. Rook Castle was dead.

"Irina," Matt said. "When you called me the other
day, I didn't get a chance to say—"

She held up a hand. "I know. Thank you, Matt." A
small, sad smile lit her face. "It's been more than two
years. It's time I stopped living in a fantasy world.

What's important now is rescuing Aimee's baby. All my resources are available to you."

He studied her face, wondering if Deke had told her about his theory that Novus was behind the kidnapping. He decided not to mention it. "I wanted to see if Deke could help me out."

"Of course. You two talk here. I need to check with Pam about my schedule. Rafe, Aaron, walk out with me."

After Irina left, Matt sat and propped his elbows on the table. He intertwined his fingers. "What's up with Rafiq? Did you talk to him about Novus?"

"He's listening in on activity around the Afghan/Pakistan/China borders. Chatter's way up in the region since Irina stopped searching." Deke rubbed his face. "Nothing concrete, mostly speculation."

"I'm glad we've got Rafe. It's good to have someone who speaks the language. Has he heard anything about what Novus is up to?"

"Well, you made big news when you left. Sounds like you're right. The chatter supports the theory that you left because you found Rook."

"Hmph. So much for my fifteen minutes of fame. I wish the chatter were right."

Deke didn't respond.

"What about you?" Matt asked him. "Are you on a case right now?" he asked.

"Nope. No case. Just hanging. I'd love to be out kicking butt somewhere, but I feel like I need to be here. You know?"

"Irina looks pretty good. How's she holding up?"

Deke shook his head. "It took a lot out of her to

make the decision to stop looking for Rook. All this time she's lived with the image of him being shot, then disappearing into the Mediterranean. It was awful—" Deke's voice cracked. "I mean, it had to have been."

Matt didn't have to imagine. He had his own night-mares. His dreams were haunted by the sight of Bill Vick spinning helplessly as he plummeted to earth, trailed by the parachute that failed to open.

"What about Aimée?" Deke continued.

"Not good. And I'm afraid I made it worse, showing up like that." Matt stared at his clasped hands. "With her about to break, and the kidnapper's demands, I've got a real situation brewing. Can you be on alert for the ransom drop?"

"Yeah, sure. When is it? Soon, I hope. There's a doozie of a winter storm heading this way, and my bird's not fond of snow."

"I know. I've been tracking the front. I think it's going to blow in earlier than they're predicting."

"You should know. I still say you should hire yourself out to the local TV station as a weatherman." It was an old joke.

"Hair gel and a blue screen? I'll do that the day you become a rodeo sharpshooter." Matt couldn't help but smile. Then he got back to business. "The ransom drop is scheduled for 1500 hours tomorrow. Here are the co-ordinates the kidnapper gave us." Matt handed Deke a scrap of paper.

Deke snagged it and stepped over to an area map hanging on the wall. He tapped the point with his finger. "It's pretty high up, and isolated."

"Yeah. I'm going to take one of our Hummers.

There's a maintenance road up the south side. It'll take at least two hours to get up there."

"I see it. But if you're right about the storm… Why don't I fly you up in the bird? It'd be a lot quicker."

"Because there's a complication. The kidnapper demanded that Aimee make the drop herself."

"The Hummer holds two passengers and it's heated. Coming back, we may have a baby."

Deke's brows shot up. "May? You don't think your kidnapper is going to turn over the kid?"

"That location gives me a bad feeling. How's he going to handle a seven-month-old, and make sure nobody gets the drop on him?"

"He'd have to have an accomplice."

"Right. That plus the storm—I don't like the odds. That's why I need you to be available. I want primary and secondary rendezvous points in case something happens and we can't use the Hummer to get out. Maybe even a tertiary." Matt paused and rubbed his neck. "The location he's picked is going to receive the brunt of that storm. He's got to know that. I have a feeling he's banking on it to cover his tracks."

"I'll have the bird ready to go."

"If you don't hear from me, head for the first rendezvous point. Be there by 0800. Here are the times and places I've got mapped out."

"Friday 0800 hours? That's sixteen hours. You're planning to ride out the storm up there? You could be blown right off that mountain."

"Thanks for that image. No. I *plan* to be back down the mountain in the Hummer with Aimee and the baby, safe and sound. The 0800 rendezvous is if we get caught by the storm or something goes wrong. If everything goes as planned, I'll call you. It'll probably be after dark."

"Just make sure you've got plenty of flares."

"Don't worry. We'll have flares. Do these times work for you?"

"Times are fine. And I see you're planning to move up toward the peak, rather than down."

"Right. I figure if we can't ride back down in the Hummer, we need to be heading to higher ground. The storm's coming in from the west. I'd like to try to stay either ahead of it or above it. Plus, your bird's not going to like dodging trees, so the fewer the better."

Deke nodded.

They quickly agreed on two alternate times and places, the second twenty-four hours after the first. Plus a third, twenty-four hours after that, in case the storm stalled.

"One last thing," Matt said. "Take these coordinates. This is a last-resort location. It's an hour's walk south from the Vicks' cabin."

"The hunting cabin. I forgot about that place. You think you might end up there?"

Matt shrugged. "It's good shelter. We might need it, if we have to travel that far."

Deke stuck the piece of paper in his pocket. "No problem. I'll hang on to these."

"Thanks, man. I knew I could count on you." Matt stood.

"You know there's another way to handle this."

"Not really."

"Sure there is. Leave Aimee out of it. You and I go

up in the Hummer, get the drop on the kidnapper and get the baby back safe and sound."

Matt sighed. "That would work—if one of us could pass for a medium-height, slender female. But there's another consideration. The baby. If everything goes well, which one of us is prepared to bring back a seven-month-old who needs his mother?"

He opened the door. "Have you ever been between a mother and her child? I'm not telling Aimee she has to stay behind."

Now Cunningham was involved.

He knew them all so well. Of course Cunningham would drop everything to help Parker. They were "brothers," after all.

It tended to get annoying, listening to the stories of their childhood friendship, and their oath to save innocents just as that broken-down Vietnam veteran had saved theirs.

He hadn't had time to sabotage Parker's equipment or vehicle. He'd had to trust Kinnard to handle that part of the plan.

His job was to make sure that when Parker needed help, it wasn't available. There were two ways he could handle that, but only one was a sure thing.

All he needed were some tools and a little private time.

FRIDAY 1430 HOURS

Aimee buried her nose more deeply into the high collar of her down parka. She'd rolled her balaclava up like a watch cap, ready to pull down over her face if she needed it. The vehicle was heated, but she was still cold.

The chill didn't come from the dropping temperatures outside, though. It came from her heart. As often as she told herself that William was safe, that the kidnapper couldn't afford to hurt him if he wanted his money, her heart remained unconvinced.

Matt's grim expression didn't help. He looked worried as he maneuvered the Hummer's steel snow tracks over the rough terrain. He glanced at her. "You okay?"

"Okay?" she croaked, then pressed her lips together. *Control,* she reminded herself. *It's all about control.* She had to hold herself together, for her baby's sake.

"If you're cold, there's a blanket under your seat."

She gave a harsh little laugh. "You think I'm worried about being *cold?*"

"Aimee, I know you're afraid something's going to happen to William. But I don't want you to neglect your own health. You're highly stressed and exhausted. You could become hypothermic without even realizing it. I need to make sure you're warm and comfortable."

"Well, don't. I don't need to be comfortable—I don't want to be. I just want to get up there, get my baby back and get home."

"That's what I want, too," Matt said.

She closed her burning eyes. *Control. Control.* She repeated it like a mantra.

"Dammit!"

She jumped and her eyes flew open.

"Sorry." His fingers tightened around the steering wheel. "I can't believe I let the kidnapper run the show. I should have jumped in and forced him to do it my way. It's dangerous for you up here."

"Where should I be? Back at home, all safe and warm? Waiting? No, thank you."

"Yes. Back at home, all safe and warm. I don't like putting you in danger. Plus, with you here, I can't do everything I'd be able to do if I were alone."

"Sorry I'm cramping your style."

"That's not—" he stopped and his jaw muscle worked. He kept his attention on the barely discernable path before them as the incline grew steeper, and the sky turned increasingly dark and gray.

Where they'd started out, near Sundance, spring was in the air, with new shoots of grass and fresh coverings of moss. As they'd climbed higher, the greenery turned brown, and patches of old snow dotted the ground.

Aimee hunched her shoulders in an effort not to shiver. Matt's hands were white-knuckled on the steering wheel. His face was expressionless, but his jaw was clamped tight. He looked the way he had the last time she'd seen him. The day he'd brought her husband's body home.

That memory spawned others. Like the argument she and Bill had a few days before that fateful day.

"It's just a weekend, Aimee. A guy trip. You're starting to sound a lot like my mother."

Aimee had yelled back at him. "Well, for once I agree with Margo. You have responsibilities here. Have you forgotten that I'm pregnant? That you're fighting cancer? Why would you want to waste even a weekend? You need to use your energy to get well. I need you to stay with me."

At that point Bill had gathered her into his arms and kissed her. "I'll be with Matt. He's safe as houses. Safer. He never takes unnecessary chances."

Then he'd looked down at her and a tender solemnity had come over his face. "Don't ever forget, Aimee. I trust Matt as much as I trust myself. More, maybe. No matter what happens, you can count on him. Ask him anything. He'll do it."

Those last words had been prophetic. Bill had asked Matt for something. Matt had obliged. And Bill had died.

The doctors had said it could have been months before the lymphoma took Bill. Long enough for him to know his child. But he'd stolen those last months from her and his son. And Matt had helped.

Then, when Aimee could have used a friend, Matt had disappeared for a year.

Bill had been wrong. She couldn't count on Matt.

"Aimee, tell me how it happened."

She started. "What? How it—?"

"The kidnapping."

"Didn't Special Agent Schiff tell you?"

He nodded. "But I'd like to hear what you remember."

Aimee closed her eyes and folded her arms. "I've been over it in my head a hundred times. I should have heard him. I should have woken up." She shook her head. "How could I have slept while someone came into my house and stole my baby?"

"William wasn't in your room, was he?"

"No. My doctor said that wasn't a good idea, for either of us. I shouldn't have listened to her. I should have kept him right beside me."

"Aimee." He put a hand on her knee. "Stop beating yourself up. You didn't do anything wrong."

His hand was warm. She could feel it even through her wool slacks and silk long underwear. She looked down.

He jerked away and gripped the steering wheel. "When did you realize he was gone?"

She was still looking at his hand. It was big and solid, with long, blunt-tipped fingers. "The sun was in my eyes, and I knew I'd overslept. William always wakes me up around five-thirty or so. He's such a sweet baby." She smiled. "He wakes up happy. I'll hear him through the monitor, cooing and laughing—" Her voice broke and her throat closed up.

He shot her a glance. "The sun woke you?" he asked gently.

"It was almost six-thirty. When I realized I hadn't heard him, I panicked. So many things can happen—"

"What did you do?"

"As soon as I realized I'd slept late, I grabbed the monitor. The camera points right at the head of the baby bed. But I couldn't see him. His bed looked empty." She took a shaky breath. "I ran across the hall. His bedroom door was open and I knew I'd left it closed. He wasn't there. He wasn't anywhere."

She felt the panic rising in her chest, heard it in her voice. Just like then. Had it only been yesterday morning?

"So I called 9-1-1."

"Schiff said there was no sign of forced entry. You're sure it was a stranger?"

Aimee frowned at Matt. "What do you mean?"

He spread his hands in a shrug without taking them off the wheel. "I just mean, is there anything specific you're thinking of when you say it was a stranger?"

She shook her head. "I just can't—it can't be anyone I know."

"Are you usually a sound sleeper?"

"No. Actually, I've been having trouble." Aimee thought about the past seven months since William Matthew's birth. All the nights she'd lain awake, worrying that something would happen to him if she went to sleep.

Dear heavens, something had.

"What about the evening before?" Matt drove steadily, watching the road and glancing occasionally into the rearview mirror. "Did you drink anything? Take anything to help you sleep?"

"No," she answered indignantly. "I would never take a chance like that with William. I gave him his bath and played with him a while, and then made myself some herbal tea and went to sleep."

Matt nodded and drove in silence for a few minutes.

Thoughts and images chased each other helter-skelter through her brain. What had she done? What had been different about that night?

"I didn't do anything differently," she said finally. "My life revolves around his, and his routine is pretty well set. I locked up the house and turned out the lights around nine, just the way I always do. I bathed him at the same time as I do every night. We played the same games we always play, then I put him to bed and went downstairs to the kitchen."

"So anyone who'd been watching the house could know almost to the minute what time you go to bed?"

Aimee nodded miserably. "Yes. My life is that ordinary. I make the same tea, use the same cup. Probably even the same spoon. I can't think of anything un-usual—" She stopped. There had been one thing differ-ent.

"What is it?"

"It's—it's nothing. It *has* to be nothing." She was really twisted—or really desperate—to even be thinking what she was thinking.

"Tell me."

"This is awful. I can't believe I'm even saying it." She took a deep breath, preparing herself for Matt's ridicule. "The tea? It's a new blend. Margo bought it for me at the health food store. They told her it was good for insomnia."

Matt glanced at her, frowning.

"But Matt, I've been drinking it every night for almost a week now."

"Is it helping you sleep?"

"Yes," she said. She hadn't really thought about it, but she *had* slept better this past week than she had in a long time. "It is. You don't think—?" Her breath hitched. "No. That's ridiculous. Margo wouldn't— Not her own—her only grandchild—" She stopped, horrified at her thoughts. During the first moments after she'd realized William was missing, she'd briefly considered that Margo might have planned it, but she'd dismissed it as impossible. She was his *grandmother.*

Matt glanced at her.

"No. She couldn't do that—could she?"

"You tell me."

"But it's outrageous. Not even Margo— I mean, yes, she's been complaining about how hard it is for her to get anything done through the Vick Corporation board since Bill died."

"What's that got to do with anything?"

"Bill left everything to William, just like his dad left everything to him. Remember when Boss Vick died?"

"Sure, that summer after we graduated from high school."

"Right. Bill was all set to go to MIT. He wanted to get his degree in aerospace engineering, then go into the Air Force, like you and Deke and Rook."

"Yeah. After his dad died, he changed his mind, and decided to go to the University of Wyoming."

"Right. To stay close to home. Margo convinced him that he had to run the business. Because when he turned twenty-one, the entire Vick Hotel fortune—and responsibility—fell into his lap."

"Bill controlled everything—"

Aimee nodded. "And Margo controlled Bill," she said bitterly.

"And now?"

"Now that Bill's dead, William stands to inherit all of it."

Matt looked at her questioningly. "What about until he's twenty-one? Who did Bill name as William's trustee?"

"Me," Aimee breathed.

"So you're the one who votes the controlling interest. That must rankle Mrs. Vick."

"I go to the board meetings, but I've never opposed a single decision. Why would I?"

"But you could."

Aimee shrugged. "I suppose. You think she did it, don't you?"

Matt glanced in the rearview mirror. "Think about it.

What does she want? What does kidnapping her own grandson right from under his mother's nose accomplish?"

"Frightening me?" Aimee cast about for any possible explanation. "Making it look like I can't—"

"Like you can't take care of your own child. What would she gain if she had custody of William? She'd retain controlling interest in the corporation. But it's damn hard to get custody away from the mother. She'd have to prove that you're unfit. That you couldn't protect your own child in your own home."

She moaned under her breath. Hearing those words in Matt's carefully neutral voice made them sound true.

"Sorry," he muttered. "But it would explain a lot."

Aimee's face felt numb. Her *mind* felt numb. Intellectually, she understood Matt's reasoning. If he were right, her mother-in-law was setting her up to take William away from her.

His words echoed in her brain, taunting her with their truth.

You couldn't protect your own child in your own home.

Chapter Three

Aimee was still reeling, still trying to process the idea that Margo could have kidnapped her baby, when she realized that Matt's demeanor had changed.

Nothing outwardly was different. His hands still held the steering wheel in a tight grip at ten and two. His expression was carefully neutral, if a bit tight.

But tension suddenly crackled in the air, and it definitely came from him.

He'd gone on alert.

"Matt, what's wrong?" she asked.

"Wrong?" He glanced in the rearview mirror.

"Don't act like you don't know what I'm talking about. Something's wrong. I can tell. Did you see something?"

He didn't reply.

His sudden transformation fascinated and frightened her. Yesterday, he'd been the consummate soldier on a mission. This morning he'd acted more like a protector. She was his charge, his responsibility.

But now in the blink of an eye, he'd morphed from protector back to predator. He was a hunter, and he'd scented his prey.

She opened her mouth to ask him again when, without warning, he veered off the stark mountain road and stopped.

"What are you doing?" Fear raced through her.

"I'll be right back," he said. "If you hear or see anything while I'm gone, lie flat across the seat. The metal should protect you."

"Protect me? Matt—?"

"Do you understand?" He glared at her, his tone and the grim set of his face brooking no argument.

"Yes," she retorted.

He walked over to the edge of the graded area and stopped at the line of trees. For a couple of seconds, he surveyed the mountain road in both directions, then reached for his fly.

Aimee gaped. Was he—? He was! On the way to exchange a million dollars for her baby, he'd stopped to take a leak! She didn't know whether to scream or laugh. Was he so confident? Or so arrogant?

She reached for the door handle, prepared to jump out and yell at him for wasting time while her child was in the hands of kidnappers. At that instant he turned his head imperceptibly to his right, back the way they'd come. And she got it—his sudden transformation. His razor-sharp alertness. Her impression that she was watching a predator.

He'd detected a threat.

Her heart jumped into her throat and she twisted in her seat, looking behind them. But she didn't see anything. Of course, she wouldn't. Matt was ex-Air Force Special Forces. His skills and senses were sharper than an ordinary person's.

She watched as he took a step closer to the trees. The sight was awesome and frightening. The curve of his back and the set of his shoulders made her think of a leopard about to spring. Standing still, he might look like a regular guy, but when he moved—*oh my.*

Absently, it occurred to her that, although she'd known Matt as long as she'd known her husband, Bill, she had almost no knowledge of his personal life or his background. He might as well be a stranger.

She hunched her shoulders, feeling fragile and human and exposed.

All at once the very air around her went still. Only the occasional snap of a twig or the rustle of bare branches in the wind broke the silence.

The nape of her neck prickled. Her pulse pounded in her ears. She didn't move, not even turning her head to glance at the spot where Matt had disappeared into the trees.

She wasn't sure how long she'd sat there, not daring to move, like a rabbit sensing a threat, when she heard it.

The crunch of twigs and rocks.

Someone was coming toward the Hummer from the opposite direction.

Without hesitation, she threw herself down across the seats, avoiding the stick shift.

It was Matt—it had to be. *Didn't it?*

She squeezed her eyes shut as the footsteps came closer. Her fingers twitched. If only she had something she could use as a weapon.

Then the driver's-side door opened.

Panic exploded in her chest and she curled her fingers into claws. Fingernails were better than nothing.

"Aimee." Matt touched her shoulder. "Good job."

Relief washed over her. Her scalp tingled. She sat up and tried to hide her trembling nerves. "You sneaked up on me," she accused.

He slid into the driver's seat. "Sorry I scared you. I wanted to circle around, make sure we weren't being watched."

"I knew you saw someone. Why couldn't you have just told me? I'd have been a lot less scared." She blew out a breath between pursed lips. "Who was it? The kidnapper?"

He shook his head and started the engine. "Can't be sure," he said shortly.

He was lying. But she'd already figured out that he would tell her just what she needed to know, and then only when she needed to know it—in *his* opinion.

Once she had William in her arms and they were safe back at home, she'd let him know what she thought about his gestapo tactics. For now, as much as she hated to admit it, his air of command, his complete confidence, and even his predatory edge, made her feel safe.

And feeling safe was dangerous.

Safety was what she longed for. But she'd learned as a child that trusting someone else to keep her safe was a fantasy. As the only child of older parents, she'd grown up with the weight of their health and safety on her shoulders.

When she'd married Bill, he'd promised to keep her safe, but he'd never been able to stand up to his mother. Then he'd promised her she could count on Matt, but he'd trusted Matt with his life, and Matt had let him die.

No. There was only one person she could count on.

Herself. She had to stay strong, stay in control. In the year since Bill's death, maintaining control was the only thing that had kept her going.

Now, at the very time when it was more important than ever to hold on to that control for her baby's sake, she was tempted to relinquish it to someone else—to Matt—and the urge scared her to death.

She lifted her chin. She was *not* going to depend on Matt. Her baby trusted her to save him.

She would.

After another fifteen minutes or so of navigating the winding mountain road, Matt pulled over again.

"What is it?" Aimee looked in the passenger-side mirror. "Did you see something again?"

He shook his head. "We're five miles from the meeting point." He pointed to the GPS locator on the dashboard. "And twenty minutes from the meeting time. So this is where I get out. I'll circle around, while you drive the rest of the way alone. You've got the case of money. You've got the baby seat, formula, diapers and blankets. The GPS locator is programmed for the exact coordinates. It's a straight shot. Just stay on this road."

He pulled a folded sheet of paper from a pocket. "Here's a printout of the route in case something happens to the GPS. You just stay on this road. Now, let's go over everything one more time."

Aimee nodded shakily. "Please. I feel like I'm in some weird dream—like all of this is a nightmare and I'm going to wake up tomorrow morning holding William."

"With any luck, that's exactly what'll happen."

His words were kind, his voice gentle. Aimee had to

clench her jaw to keep from crying. Time stretched out before her like an endless road. It would be hours before she'd be back home with William, safe and sound. Many hours and many opportunities for something to go wrong.

"Hey, Aimee," Matt said. He lifted a hand toward her cheek, then checked the movement. "It's going to be okay."

She lifted her chin. "Don't do that. Don't spout meaningless promises to me. I need to know what I'm up against. What if the kidnapper doesn't bring William? What if my baby's cold, or hungry—?" She bit her cheek. *Control,* she reminded herself.

"Whoa. You can't worry about any of that. And remember, being scared is normal. You're very brave."

"Oh, yeah. I'm the bravest woman on the planet, driving up this remote mountain to rescue my baby from a kidnapper." Tears stung her eyes and a lump lodged in her throat.

She was so *not* brave.

"Matt. I'm so scared." She touched his sleeve, and then squeezed the material in her fist.

A tender look softened his sculpted features. "Listen to me. You *are* the bravest woman on the planet. And—" He paused for a second. "Bill was the luckiest man in the universe. Aimee, I—"

"Don't—" She stiffened and held up her hands. "Please. Don't start. I have to think about William. I can't afford to get all emotional about what happened to Bill."

Matt's expression closed down. He nodded. "Yeah. Best to hate me for one thing at a time," he said flatly.

She caught what appeared to be sadness in his dark

eyes before he averted his gaze. His words and the look surprised her. It wasn't like Matt to feel sorry for himself.

He shrugged it off and climbed out of the Hummer, pulling a daypack out with him. Then he leaned his forearms on the driver's-side door. "I put on the emergency brake. Don't forget to release it before you head out."

"I've ridden ATVs in these hills all my life. I can handle this Hummer."

He nodded matter-of-factly. "I've got my route planned out. Going straight up, it'll take me about fifteen to twenty minutes to reach the rendezvous point. If you drive no faster than fifteen miles per hour, we should arrive at about the same time, since this maintenance road snakes back and forth, and the terrain is getting rougher. Just stay on it. Don't get lost."

"I'll be fine."

"Aimee, I can't stress too strongly how dangerous this man could be. If anything—*anything*—goes wrong, you have to turn the Hummer around and head down the mountain as fast as you can. With or without William. Understand?"

"No. I don't understand. There's no way I'm going anywhere without my baby."

"Listen to me. I *have* to know that you'll do as I say. I promise you, you won't have to deal with him. I'm going to ambush him. I don't expect anything to go wrong, but if something does, I have to know you'll follow my orders. Do what I say. I can't do my job—I can't rescue William—if I have to worry about you. Your baby will be safe. I swear."

Aimee frowned, studying his face. There was something else—something he wasn't telling her. He wouldn't meet her gaze. Instead, he stared down at his clasped hands.

Suddenly she understood. "You don't think he's bringing William, do you?"

His head ducked lower for an instant. Then he straightened.

"Do you?" Aimee grabbed his hand before he could remove it from the car door. She held on until he bent down again. His dark eyes finally met hers—solemn, guarded.

"Oh—" Her heart cracked wide open and all her careful efforts at control spilled out. She shook her head slowly, back and forth, back and forth. "No, please, Matt. Tell me my baby's okay."

He reached out and brushed a strand of hair from her cheek. "Aimee, I swear to God, if I have to die to make it happen, William will be back in your arms today, safe and sound."

THE MAN WAS LIGHTER on his feet than Matt had expected, given his size and the bulky daypack strapped to his back. His clothes and pack were a winter camouflage pattern that blended perfectly into the patchy snow and barren trees as he moved.

And he moved well, silently as a woodland animal, alert to everything around him. An assault rifle—military grade—was hooked over one shoulder.

Matt could tell he was ex-military. Maybe even ex-Special Forces. That explained this location, the timing and the man's obvious comfort in his surroundings. Not many people knew how to glide silently through rough terrain, leaving almost no trail.

Matt would bet money that he was also a survivalist. He had to have trekked every inch of this mountain, or he wouldn't have chosen it.

But was he here alone?

Matt had no doubt that he'd seen sunlight glinting off metal in the Hummer's rearview mirror as the vehicle had snaked back and forth up the maintenance road. That was why he'd stopped, to try and catch a glimpse of whoever was tailing them. But he hadn't spotted anything.

Whoever was back there was good. Probably as good as the man in front of him. Impressively close to having Matt's own skills.

The question in Matt's mind was—were there two guys following him? This man could have followed them up the road and then cut through just as Matt had and beaten him to the ransom drop point.

But it was also possible that he had an accomplice, and the accomplice had followed them while this guy waited up here.

Matt couldn't afford to let down his guard, so until he knew otherwise, he assumed the kidnapper had an accomplice.

Matt had to watch his back.

He'd planned out as much of his strategy as he could. He, too, was dressed in winter camo and carried a small daypack. Besides binoculars, he was equipped with a compact MAC-10 machine pistol he didn't plan on using, a mini-tranquilizer gun and a few flexicuffs.

His intent was to surprise the kidnapper and immobilize him with the tranq gun. Once he had him restrained, he could definitely make it worth his while to reveal the baby's location.

He crouched, hidden by scrubby bushes, and observed the kidnapper through his high-powered binoculars. The man was positioning himself for greatest cover and widest angle of sight.

For a couple of seconds, Matt held his breath, listening for the Hummer's engine, but he didn't hear anything. It was nerve-racking, waiting up here, knowing Aimee was about to drive straight into the lion's den. All this would be so much easier if he didn't have to worry about her being hurt.

Matt shifted, examining the area around the kidnapper. He searched for signs of another person—someone whose job it was to take care of the baby. He used a careful mental grid layout he'd developed in the Air Force.

The controlled search made it impossible to miss a person, much less a vehicle, but all Matt saw was a set of tracks made by a one-man snowmobile. He saw no trace of the vehicle itself. The kidnapper had done a damn good job of hiding his vehicle and covering his tracks.

Matt's respect for him went up a notch, and his fear for Aimee's baby went up three. The suspicion that had planted itself in his brain from the first moment he'd seen the TV news, rooted itself more deeply, undermining his confidence.

If this man were simply a kidnapper, out to make a quick million, and if he'd come to make a good-faith exchange, then why didn't he have the baby?

Matt continued his grid search until he'd covered every square inch of visible land surface. He saw nothing that indicated anyone but the kidnapper had been—or was—in the area. He pocketed the binoculars.

Damn. He would hate to be right about this one.

Although the kidnapper seemed to be all about money, and Aimee's revelations about Margo's need to control the Vick Corporation made Margo a prime suspect, Matt didn't believe it.

A silent vibration started near his left knee. His cell phone. Grimacing, he shifted enough to pull it out of the cargo pocket of his camo pants. Keeping one eye on the kidnapper, he glanced at the screen.

It was a text message from Deke. He focused on the letters.

GOT PSNGR LIST OF YR FLIGHT. HAFIZ AL HAMAR, AFGH NATL, ON IT. SEE PHOTO. DC.

It only took a couple of seconds for the photo to come through. Matt cursed silently when he saw it. He'd seen that man before. He'd run into him several times in Mahjidastan.

Still watching the kidnapper, Matt keyed in a quick message back to Deke and, making sure the sound was off on his phone, hit SEND.

RECOG AL HAMAR FR MAHJID. TRACE HIM? MP

A sick certainty burned in the pit of his gut. Novus Ordo had engineered William's kidnapping to get his hands on Matt, to interrogate him about whether Rook was alive. And that meant he wanted Matt alive. But Matt was sure Novus wouldn't blink at killing anyone who got in his way.

Matt had made a huge mistake by bringing Aimee up here. He should have come alone, or brought Deke or another BHSAR specialist.

If he was right about Novus, and he was becoming more and more sure about that by the hour, she and her baby were disposable pawns in an international terrorist's effort to protect his identity.

The kidnapper was on the move again. Matt pocketed his phone and cleared his mind. He needed focus and hair-trigger response. If he failed to return William Matthew to his mother's arms, he'd have plenty of time for regrets and unbearable sorrow later. His mission was to get the drop on the kidnapper and rescue Aimee's baby. He didn't allow the thought that William wasn't here to enter his head. He had to operate as if he were.

He crouched in a position from which he could spring in a fraction of a second, and let his senses feed him information. They were as clear as the mountain air. The smell of evergreen and the coming snow teased his nostrils. The tingling in his hands and face signaled the dropping temperature.

And the quickly darkening sky telegraphed the approach of the winter storm—early, just as he'd predicted.

The only sound Matt heard was the rustling of bare tree branches and evergreen needles in the rising wind.

The kidnapper raised his head, as if sniffing a scent on the breeze. He appeared calm and relaxed, and yet poised to react with swift reflexes.

Damn, the man was good.

A discordant hum rose in the distance. The Hummer. Aimee was almost here. The kidnapper swung the rifle from his shoulder and settled into a comfortable, balanced stance—observant and attentive—ready for anything.

Matt shifted, feeling the weight of the MAC-10 in its holster. He could get to it if necessary, but he didn't plan on using it. He held the tranq gun and the flexicuffs were looped through his belt.

The Hummer's engine grew louder, its steady roar filling the air around them. The engine's noise blocked Matt's keen hearing, but it also covered any noise he might make when he sneaked up on the kidnapper.

After an automatic glance around, Matt crept forward, until he was less than twenty feet behind the man. With his tactical-grade, compression-fit long underwear, he had far greater agility than the bulkily dressed kidnapper. He could rush him, sink a tranq dart in his neck and cuff him within seconds.

The Hummer crested the rise, and Matt's pulse kicked into high gear. He could barely make out Aimee's silhouette through the vehicle's tinted windows. As he watched, she slowed down, then rolled to a stop.

Stay in the vehicle. Make him come to you. He silently recited the instructions he'd given her.

He'd retrofitted a loudspeaker for her to use for any necessary communications. He'd warned her not to exit the vehicle until the kidnapper produced the baby. And, as he'd reminded her not twenty minutes before, at the first sign of trouble, she was to turn the Hummer around and get out of there.

Those were *her* instructions. But Matt had other plans. He had no intention of letting the kidnapper within twenty yards of her.

She inched the Hummer closer. The kidnapper shifted to the balls of his feet, holding the rifle loosely yet competently, like a pro. Another point in his favor and more cause for concern on Matt's part.

Matt made his move. He rose from his crouch and crept around the edge of the clearing, keeping the scrub bushes between him and the other man. Once he got into position, it would take him less than thirty seconds to get behind him, slip out from the trees at the last second, then grab and tranquilize him. In a situation like this, thirty seconds was a hell of a long time.

He'd choreographed every step ahead of time. He'd had plenty of experience with stealth from rescue missions he'd conducted in the Air Force and afterwards while working for Black Hills Search and Rescue. He knew how to approach an enemy and extract an innocent without detection. Given this guy's obvious expertise, he was glad to have the noise of the Hummer's engine as added cover.

He positioned himself directly behind the kidnapper. Staying low, he inched silently forward.

Then without warning, something hit him from behind.

With no more than a fifth of a second wasted on startle response, Matt whirled. He rammed his fist and shoulder into the attacker's body. As his knuckles encountered flesh and bone, he followed through, putting his whole weight behind the blow. But it wasn't enough. His attacker was quicker.

Matt went down—hard.

The man grabbed a handful of his hair and slammed his face into the frozen ground.

The blow dazed him. But the cold pressure of a gun barrel pressed to the side of his neck brought him back instantaneously. Adrenaline sheared his breath and cleared his brain. He jerked just as a quiet pop echoed in his ear. Something sharp scratched his neck.

A pop. Not a bullet. A tranquilizer dart.

Damn! Even as the thoughts rushed through his brain, he torpedoed his elbow backward. With a breathy grunt, the man fell away and his tranq gun went flying.

Before he hit the ground, Matt whirled and grabbed his collar. With a renewed burst of energy, and using muscles he hadn't used in months, Matt heaved the man's bulk around, between himself and the kidnapper.

Pocketing his own tranquilizer gun, Mat slid the MAC-10 from its holster and buried its barrel into the flesh of his attacker's neck. He was tempted to rip off the man's ski mask, but to do that, he'd have to let go of the man or the gun.

"You nearly got me with your tranq dart, but believe me, this is not a tranq gun," he growled, scanning the area in front of him in case the kidnapper had heard them. "It's the real thing. And it will take your head clean off if you don't tell me who you are."

His answer was a blood-chilling string of curses, some English, some Arabic. Dammit, the kidnapper had to have heard him.

"Are you *Al Hamar?*"

The man's head jerked in surprise.

"So—you are. Did Novus Ordo send you?" Matt whispered, digging the muzzle of the MAC-10 deeper into his flesh.

His prisoner shook his head, but Matt saw the truth in the man's black eyes. "Tell me what you know about the kidnapping—"

The crack of exploding gunpowder hit his ears a fraction of a second before the bullet whistled past his head.

Matt ducked.

Al Hamar used Matt's own elbow trick to knock the wind out of him, then leapfrogged across three or four feet of ground, diving for his own weapon. The kidnapper shot again.

Matt aimed the machine pistol at Al Hamar. But something was wrong. He couldn't clear his vision. He bent his head and squeezed his eyes shut for an instant. Just as he did, a second bullet grazed his ear.

He swallowed a pained cry and his hand flew to his ear. It came away bloody. His bloodstained fingers trembled as he stared at the proof of how close the bullet had come. If he hadn't paused to clear his vision, it would have split his skull.

A high-pitched scream, barely distinguishable above the roar of the Hummer's engine, sent his heart slamming into his chest. It was Aimee. She gunned the engine and the vehicle shot forward, toward the kidnapper.

Aimee, no! What was she doing? *Turn around. Get out of here.*

The kidnapper aimed at the Hummer's windshield.

At the same time, Matt saw Al Hamar whirl around, brandishing a semiautomatic pistol.

Matt ducked down and rubbed his eyes. The scratch on his neck had absorbed some of the tranquilizer. Enough to blur his vision. He cursed silently and gave his head a quick shake.

The kidnapper yelled something that Matt didn't catch, then several bullets thunked into a tree to Matt's left. He was shooting at Al Hamar again.

So, they weren't working together.

Al Hamar yelped and toppled forward.

When Matt looked back at the kidnapper, the high-powered gun was aimed at his head. From that distance, the man couldn't miss. But before Matt could react and dive, he swung back toward the Hummer.

Why hadn't he shot him? He might not get as good a chance again.

Rising to a crouch, Matt took a precious split second to make sure his head was as clear as possible, then sprinted toward the Hummer, spraying bullets on the ground in front of the kidnapper. He couldn't kill the man. He needed him alive—at least long enough to find out where William was being held.

As he crouched behind a stand of bushes, he heard the hitch in the engine noise that signaled shifting gears.

Good, Aimee! Now turn around and get out of here!

But a Hummer didn't turn on a dime, or even a quarter. Still, she was trying.

Careful to stay hidden, he lifted his head just in time to see the kidnapper raise his weapon and aim at the Hummer's windshield.

Alarm ripped through him. The kidnapper was about to shoot Aimee. The high-powered blast would be enough to penetrate the tempered glass.

Matt raised his weapon, his breath catching as his finger sought the hair-trigger of the MAC-10.

Aimee would hate him if he shot the man who could lead them to her baby. But if he had to kill the kidnapper to save Aimee, then so be it. He'd find her baby some other way.

Chapter Four

Just as Matt's finger started to squeeze the trigger, the kidnapper lowered the barrel of his gun to the tires.

Matt's scalp tingled with relief. At least he was no longer aiming at Aimee. Still, he had to stop him from disabling their only means of getting down the mountain. He vaulted to his feet, brandishing the MAC.

"Hey!" he shouted. "You want your money? Then stop now! Or you'll never see it."

He swayed, but immediately caught himself. Blinking away the haze that threatened to obscure his vision, he yelled, "In fact, you'll never see tomorrow!"

He strafed the ground in front of the kidnapper. But the other man didn't take the bait. His rifle barrel didn't even waver. He fired.

A tire exploded with a loud crack.

A second shot. A second crack.

The Hummer rocked dizzily, then tilted to the passenger side. It was going over.

Aimee!

Matt loosed another volley of bullets, closer this time. He still hadn't ruled out killing the man.

The shooter dove for the ground. But in one smooth motion, he righted himself and fired again—this time at the Hummer's gas tank. Metallic thunks peppered the vehicle's frame.

Wincing each time the kidnapper shot, Matt tried to draw a bead on him, but the kidnapper's duck and roll had positioned the Hummer between them.

Matt sprinted toward the vehicle. He had to stop him. It was only a matter of seconds before a bullet hit the gas tank.

Suddenly, the man stopped shooting, slung his rifle over his shoulder and ran toward the disabled vehicle.

He was going after the money.

Matt had to stop him before he got to Aimee. He broke into a run. His legs pumped, his heart raced. The earth and the sky went topsy-turvy and he stumbled, but he recovered his footing and kept going.

The tranquilizer was doing more than turn Matt's world upside down, though. His legs were as heavy as lead weights. It was like a bad dream. As hard as he pushed, he couldn't beat the other man.

The kidnapper vaulted up the vehicle's undercarriage like a free climber and ripped open the driver's-side door.

Reaching in, he grabbed Aimee's parka and yanked her up and out through the door. She struggled, but she was no match for the big man. He shoved her over the side. Then he dove back down and popped out immediately with the briefcase.

By the time Matt rounded the rear of the Hummer, the kidnapper was back on the ground.

Finally, Matt had a clean shot. He stopped and took aim, blinking rapidly. He wanted to disable him without killing him.

But Aimee's crumpled form filled his wavering vision. She was lying near the Hummer. Too near. Her feet were mere inches from the widening puddle of gasoline.

The kidnapper seemed preoccupied with the briefcase, but Matt couldn't count on that. In one stride he'd be close enough to grab her. He could use her as a shield.

Or kill her.

Swallowing against dizziness brought on by the tranq, Matt carefully tightened his finger on the trigger.

Aimee stirred and moaned, distracting him for a split second. When he turned his full attention back to the kidnapper, the man had produced an old-fashioned silver cigarette lighter in his hand. He flipped open the lid.

Matt aimed at his right shoulder, concentrating on keeping the sights of the machine pistol steady.

Aimee sat up. The kidnapper's sharp gaze met Matt's as he stepped backward and sideways, putting her between himself and Matt. He crouched down, making himself too small a target to hit without endangering Aimee.

As Matt watched helplessly, he nodded at him, then struck the lighter and tossed it over Aimee's head and into the middle of the pool of gasoline.

The small flame looped through the air as if in slow motion. When it was a couple of inches above the puddle, the fumes caught and flared. By the time the lighter splashed into the liquid gasoline, the flames were two feet high and spreading.

The kidnapper turned and sprinted away to the east.

Matt couldn't worry about him. The fire was growing, and flames were rising only inches from Aimee's legs.

"Aimee, get back!" he yelled.

She scrambled backward, her eyes wide and bright with terror.

Pocketing his gun, Matt rushed toward her. A shot rang out—but not from the direction in which the kidnapper had run.

It came from the south. *Al Hamar.* Matt dove the last few feet. He landed next to Aimee as red flames licked at her hiking boots.

Scooping his hands under her arms, he lifted her and heaved her as far as he could and then dove on top of her, covering her body with his, shielding her head with his hands.

Behind them, the flames roared and spit like a massive beast. The ground trembled beneath them and a whistling sound filled the air.

The flares! He'd packed a dozen of them into the rear of the Hummer.

"What's that?" Aimee whispered.

"It's okay," he whispered. "You're okay. Just stay still." Matt hunched his shoulders and pressed his cheek against hers, doing his best to shield every inch of her body with his. He could feel her panicked breaths against his cheek, hear them sawing in and out through her throat. He could smell the lemon sweetness of her hair.

She stopped wriggling and turned her head a little more, which put her lips about an inch away from his. He closed his eyes and pretended they weren't there.

He couldn't tell how many of the flares fired because suddenly, with a deafening roar, the gasoline exploded.

For an instant, the air grew totally still and quiet, as the conflagration sucked in oxygen. Then a blast of heat strafed them, like the breath of a fire-breathing dragon. Matt felt the sting of heat across the backs of his hands and the nape of his neck.

After several seconds, he lifted his head slightly and peeked at the Hummer. It was still engulfed in flames, but they were weakening.

Their supplies and equipment. He stiffened, and felt Aimee move beneath him.

"Matt?"

"Stay still," he commanded. He rose to a crouch with his weapon drawn and rapidly scanned the clearing, but they were alone. The kidnapper and Al Hamar gone.

He turned back to Aimee. "Why didn't you turn the Hummer around and get out of here like I told you to?"

"He shot you!" she hissed. "I saw you go down. I thought you were dead. I had to save my baby."

He held her gaze for a moment, wanting to berate her for endangering her life by not obeying him, but she lifted her chin and stared at him with defiance in her eyes.

It occurred to him that there was probably no emotion in humans stronger than the one radiating from her. The fierceness of the love of a woman for her child.

There was no way he could counter that.

Setting the machine pistol down, he shrugged his daypack off his shoulders.

"What are you doing?" she asked.

Ignoring her, he quickly assessed his clothing. Had

he landed in gasoline when he dove for Aimee? He didn't see any stains, and didn't smell gas.

"Don't move," he said, pointing at the ground where she sat. "I'm going to see if I can salvage anything out of the Hummer."

"You can't go near that," Aimee said. "Wait until the fire dies down."

He shook his head. By the time the flames died down there would be nothing left. Hell, there was probably nothing left anyhow.

He approached the burning vehicle cautiously.

Everything inside was black and smoldering, or still burning. By the red-and-yellow flickering light, he saw what was left of the baby seat, melted down to a nearly unrecognizable lump of plastic. Behind it, in the back of the vehicle, he could see the damage caused by the flares that he'd packed to help Deke set his helicopter down in the dark.

Then he spotted his backpack. There was nothing left of his supplies and equipment. The nylon webbing that crisscrossed its lightweight frame had burned and melted.

Matt cursed silently. Everything he'd packed so carefully—planning for any contingency—was burned and useless. His double sleeping bag, the concentrated nutrient packs, rain gear, snowshoes, spare batteries for the GPS locator and phone, first aid kit, even the water canteens, were gone.

He sucked in a deep breath, and coughed as smoke scalded his throat. It was getting thicker and blacker as the flames died.

There was still plenty of heat, which would have come in handy if it weren't almost certainly toxic, judging by the smell. Between the upholstery, the gasoline, oil and other fluids, and the various plastics and dyes, there was no telling how contaminated the air was.

They couldn't stay near that fire.

He headed back to where Aimee was waiting.

She took a breath to speak, and coughed when she got a lungful of smoke. She took his hand and let him help her stand.

She looked over her shoulder. "I need to get my bag. William's baby food and diapers and—"

"They're gone. Burned up. My supplies are, too. We'll have to make do."

"But—"

"Come on. We need to get away from here. That smoke is toxic."

Aimee coughed again, proving his point. She looked up at him and gasped. "Oh! Matt, you're bleeding. It's all over your face and neck."

He touched his ear and winced, then looked at his hand. A fresh smear of blood stained his finger. "Don't worry. I'm okay," he said shortly, as a wave of dizziness reminded him just how handicapped he still was by the tranquilizer.

"Hell, another quarter inch and the bullet would have missed me completely."

Aimee pushed his hand away and stood on tiptoe, looking at the wound. "That's not funny," she snapped.

She touched the curve of his ear, near the raw scrape. "It looks like the bleeding has almost stopped."

He shrugged away her touch. It took concentration to ignore the gentle brush of her fingers.

"Stand behind me." He held the pistol waist high and swept the clearing with it and his gaze.

She grasped his sleeve and pointed toward the east. "He ran into the woods in that direction. We've got to go after him."

Matt twisted away from her grip and put a hand on her shoulder. "He's long gone. The fire gave him a big head start."

"No! We've got to go. We have to catch up—"

"Aimee. He's twenty minutes ahead of us. It's getting dark. We'll never catch up to him tonight."

She turned and stared at him, the brightness of her green eyes fading as understanding dawned. Her hands covered her mouth. A stray flake of snow caught on her lashes.

"But—he got the money," she cried. "And he's still got William. He doesn't need my baby any longer. What if—"

A giant fist squeezed his heart at the utter desolation on her face—in her voice. He opened his mouth to lie, to feed her false hope. "We'll find him, Aimee. Don't worry—"

"Don't worry? Don't—?" She gulped in a desperate breath. "He's my *baby*. He's so little. He's only seven months old. He will *die* without me."

She doubled her hands into fists. "Don't tell me not to worry!" she screamed.

He steeled himself for her attack, figuring she had a perfect right. He hadn't kept his word. He'd let both men get the best of him. One had sneaked up on him because he'd let his guard down. The other had turned his own equipment into a weapon against him.

But she didn't. She pressed her fists to her eyes. "What do we do now?" she whispered.

Matt gently pulled her hands away from her face. Then he touched her chin. "Aimee. Look at me."

She raised her gaze to his, and he winced at the unbearable sorrow in her eyes.

"The kidnapper doesn't have the money," he said.

Aimee's eyes went round. "What?"

"We put a few thousand dollars in the briefcase, on top. But as soon as he digs down a few layers, all he'll find is scrap paper."

"He doesn't have—?" Aimee's pale cheeks flared with pink. She sent Matt an incredulous smile.

Matt shook his head. "I've got it here, in the daypack. If he'd given William to you, I'd have given him the pack."

"He doesn't have the money," she said in awe.

Matt nodded. "That's right."

"So he *has* to take care of my baby until he gets it." *If the money is what he's after.*

For an instant he allowed himself to bask in the joy on her face. Then a flake of snow drifted past her cheek, followed by another, and another.

He looked toward the west. The sky was dark with thick, gray clouds. He grimaced and shivered as a fat snowflake slipped down the back of his neck.

Where was his parka? There, on the ground near the woods.

"We'd better get going," he said as he went over to get it. "The storm's heading this way. As soon as it's over I'll call Deke and we'll—" He bent over to pick up the parka, and suddenly the world turned upside down—several times. His knee hit the hard ground with a painful thud.

"Matt?"

He jerked his head up. Her blurry, wavering face filled his vision.

"Matt! What's wrong?"

He held up a hand. With more than a little effort he closed his fist around the down-filled jacket and pushed himself to his feet. "I'm okay. I got a little dose of a tranquilizer dart when the second guy grabbed me. It's almost worn off."

"Tranquilizer dart?" Aimee's smile faded. "I don't understand. Why did the kidnappers need a tranquilizer dart?"

He rubbed his eyes and shook his head.

But she wouldn't let it go. "I don't understand. These men, these kidnappers—why bring all those weapons—" She stopped, her eyes narrowing.

"Why did *you* need a machine gun?"

When he met her gaze, his throat spasmed, and that punishing fist tightened and twisted until his heart wanted to burst. But before he could answer, she lifted her chin.

"Okay. Let me make it easier on you. Just answer this one question for me. The question you never answered yesterday. How did you happen to show up back in Wyoming just in time to be available when William was kidnapped?" she asked.

"What?" Matt answered automatically.

"You. Heard. Me." A muscle ticked in her jaw and her nostrils flared. She took a step toward him, holding his gaze. "I woke up at six-thirty yesterday morning to find that my baby had been abducted from right under my nose. And then before noon you showed up." She pressed her fingertips to her mouth for a second. "You must have been here for days, or—or weeks for all I know."

Matt swallowed. "I flew in Tuesday night."

She nodded shakily. "Not even two days." She looked away, as if composing herself, and then looked at him again. "Why?"

"Why what?"

"Matt, stop it. Why did you fly back here on Tuesday, and my baby was kidnapped on Wednesday? Am I supposed to believe that was a *coincidence?*"

"Aimee, I don't know what you're thinking—" He was lying again. He knew exactly what she was thinking.

What was the connection?

"Answer me."

More snowflakes fell. The storm was almost upon them. By sheer force of will, he stopped himself from examining the sky. Aimee needed as much assurance as he could give her right now—which admittedly wasn't much.

"I came back to Wyoming because Irina called me back. She had to stop looking for Rook."

Aimee's mouth fell open. "Had to stop? Oh, no. I didn't think she would ever give up. She must be devastated."

He nodded. "She is. But she can't do it anymore. She's out of money."

A little frown appeared between her brows. "She called you last week?"

He nodded, wondering what she was thinking. She didn't have the information he and Deke had. She knew nothing about Rook's relationship with Novus Ordo, or the threat he'd posed to the mysterious terrorist as long as he was alive.

"These men—"

"Aimee, I don't know either of them."

She shook her head slowly. "They don't have William, do they? This isn't about my baby at all." Her hands pressed against her chest, as if trying to stop the pain.

"Oh, dear heavens," she gasped. "That other man— he wasn't speaking English."

"I don't know them—" he repeated, but she cut him off with a gesture.

"But you know who they are, don't you?" she snapped. "They have something to do with whatever you've been doing overseas. They followed you back here to Wyoming. Somehow, they knew they could get to you by kidnapping my baby."

"Aimee, don't—"

"They don't care about William. They want you," she whispered. "For all you know, my baby is dead."

Chapter Five

Matt caught Aimee's shoulders as she swayed. "Listen to me," he said firmly.

She steadied herself by closing her fingers around the sleeves of his sweater.

"William is still alive. I know he is." Dear God, he hoped she believed him. The reticence in his voice was painfully obvious to him.

She looked at him, her eyes filled with doubt and despair. Slowly, a little of the anguish faded from her expression. "Do you really think so?"

He forced his stiff lips to smile. "I know so. I swear, Aimee, I have no idea who these men are, but you saw the way the kidnapper grabbed the briefcase and ran. He couldn't wait to get to the money."

Dear God, he hoped his desperate explanation sounded plausible.

He took a deep breath. "But he's going to find out that we outsmarted him. And now we've seen him. We can identify him. He can't afford to let anything happen to William now."

He did his best not to wince. He wasn't sure if it was

the tranquilizer circulating in his blood, or the desperation clouding his brain, but his reasoning had holes so big he could have driven the Hummer through them if it hadn't burned up.

He prayed that Aimee wasn't thinking rationally enough to dispute him. Right now what she needed was reassurance, not raw truth.

And she certainly didn't need to know that he echoed her suspicions. He wasn't sure who either of the men were, but he knew there was more going on than just the kidnapping of a baby for money.

He shook his head, trying to shake off the tranquilizer's effect, and another snowflake slid inside the neck of his sweater.

He looked up at the sky. The clouds were dark, feeding the dropping temperature. Within an hour, the sun would go down, and then the mercury would plummet. They were running out of time.

He had to make a decision. Several, if he could remember what they were. A lungful of icy air helped to clear his head.

He glanced at his watch and then stared at the tangle of briar bushes where he'd last seen the terrorist who'd followed him from Mahjidastan. He had to check on him.

He knew the man was wounded. He'd heard him shriek when the kidnapper's bullet had hit him. But after that the terrorist had fired a shot. Had that been the last brave effort of a dying man? Or a parting shot before he escaped to lick his wound? He had to find out.

Good. He rubbed his temples. At least he finally had come to a decision.

"Aimee, get over here and stay behind me. I need to

check the area, in case Al Hamar is wounded or dead, and I don't want to let you out of my sight."

"Al Hamar?" Her eyes widened, then immediately narrowed. "You know his name? I thought you said you didn't know either of them."

He sighed and spread his hands. "I don't. I got a text message from Deke, telling me—" He stopped. "It's complicated, Aimee. I just need you to trust me."

She shook her head slowly. "Do I have any choice?"

"No," he said grimly. "Have you ever shot a pistol before?"

"No. Rifles, shotguns, bows and arrows. But not a pistol." She sounded like she was about to cry.

"It's okay. This is a Glock." He pulled the small handgun out of his daypack and handed it to her. "It's loaded, and it doesn't have a safety, so it's ready to shoot. You pull the trigger the same way you do a rifle. And you hold it in both hands, like the cops on TV. Okay?"

"I think so."

"Trust me, you probably won't have to use it. But I need to know—can you shoot a man if you have to?"

She lifted her chin. "Will it help me get William back? Then, yes, I can."

"Okay. Stay directly behind me. By now the guy's either dead or long gone. But there's no way I'm leaving the area until I verify that he's not waiting to ambush us."

Aimee met his gaze. "I'm ready."

The determination in her expression told him she meant it. To his surprise, something welled up in his chest until it almost cut off his breath. Her bravery and trust awed and scared him.

"Good," he said roughly. "Let's go."

He held the MAC-10 at waist level, ready to shoot if necessary, as he moved cautiously toward the bushes. A couple of feet away, he held up his hand.

"Wait here. Remember what I told you in the car? Same goes here. If you hear anything—anything at all—hit the dirt. Copy?"

"Yes."

He crouched and crept forward to the edge of the patch. Peering through the tangle of bare briar-studded vines didn't work. They were too thick. He straightened, weapon at the ready, and moved close enough to see over the tops.

The briar bushes covered about four feet of ground. Beyond that he saw new scrapes and crushed twigs and leaves.

Glancing back at Aimee, he drew a circle in the air with his left hand. "I'm circling around," he mouthed, then held up his palm. "You stay there."

She nodded carefully.

He circled the bushes and bent to study the scrapes on the ground. In among the dried leaves and twigs, Matt saw a saucer-sized pool of blood. Beyond it, dark red drops drew a path toward the trees, like bread crumbs left by Hansel and Gretel.

"He's wounded, but not fatally. He got away." He followed the trail of blood toward the trees, dividing his attention between the ground and the wooded area ahead of him.

At the edge of the clearing, he stopped. For a few seconds, he stood still, listening for the sound of a motor, but all he heard was the wind rustling the bare branches. Carefully, he followed the blood trail for a few more steps, until the underbrush was too thick to penetrate, and the tree's roots met and intertwined on the ground.

He backed away, staying in his own footsteps until he reached the stand of bushes. When he turned, he nearly ran into Aimee.

"When I tell you to stay put, you've got to stay put," he said sternly, wishing he felt like smiling at her determined stance.

She stood, legs apart, holding the Glock like every cop on *Law & Order,* although her expression more closely resembled that of a terrified witness.

"The kidnapper definitely wounded him. He's losing a good bit of blood. I don't think he'll try anything else. If he's got any sense, and if he's got a vehicle—which I'm sure he does—he's probably headed down the mountain by now."

"What do we do now?" she asked.

He frowned. "If I had the Hummer, I'd send you down to it. But without it we're not going anywhere, except to find a way to get you out of this storm."

Aimee shivered and hunched her shoulders against the wind. She was already feeling the cold, even in her down parka and balaclava.

His insulated underwear was keeping him warm. If he thought it would help her, he'd strip it off and give it to her. But the suit had been custom-fitted to his body for maximum insulation. It would be much too large for her, and therefore useless. Besides, if he were going to keep her safe, he had to keep himself warm and mobile.

Aimee still held the Glock. He put on his parka and

lifted the daypack onto his shoulders. Then he took the Glock and stowed it in a side pocket.

After glancing up at the sky one more time, he pulled the satellite phone out of his pocket and looked at it. No signal.

Why was he not surprised?

He wasn't sure if the problem was the cloud cover or the cold, but it didn't matter. There would be no nighttime rescue tonight. He couldn't contact Deke or anyone else until the storm passed.

He put the phone away and pulled out the GPS locator. *Again, no satellite reception.* He'd have to rely on old-fashioned methods of finding his way. He'd memorized the maps, so he knew where they were going. He just hoped they could make it before the storm caught up to them in full force.

It was almost 1900 hours. Seven o'clock. They had, at best, thirty minutes of daylight left. A stab of apprehension pierced his chest. He'd mapped out three shelters within reasonable distance of the ransom drop point. The one closest to his primary rendezvous point was 4.8 miles, heading 41 degrees, almost directly east. The next closest to rendezvous was 4.5 miles at 18 degrees.

The third shelter would be the easiest walk. It was two miles away, but the direction was 30 degrees, which put it farthest from the primary rendezvous point.

He could picture the grid in his head. If he were alone, he'd head directly for the primary shelter. A hike of 4.8 miles would be less than an hour at his usual pace, even in snow.

But he figured Aimee could cover about three miles per hour at best, and that didn't take the snowstorm into consideration. It would take her almost two hours. Which wouldn't be so much of a problem if they'd gotten started an hour earlier.

But they hadn't. And as he'd feared, the storm was moving in at least three hours ahead of predictions, just as he'd told Special Agent Schiff. So he had no choice but to head for the nearest shelter, even if it was farthest from the primary rendezvous point.

"How far do we have to go?" Aimee asked, as if she were reading his mind.

"With any luck we can make it in an hour or a little more," he said, knowing he was being optimistic. The longer it took, the harder it would be. He could smell the snow in the air and he figured the wind was already up to twelve miles per hour. His prediction was that it would reach fifty miles per hour or more before the storm played out. And Matt didn't want to be caught outside in it.

He sure as hell didn't want Aimee exposed. Once they made it to the shelter, they could get a good night's sleep and get an early start.

Plus, as soon as the storm moved out, he could contact Deke and arrange a new, closer rendezvous point. He could tell Deke to bring replacement gear and supplies, and pick up Aimee.

He shook his head. Getting Aimee to leave without her baby was going to be a trick. Surely two ex-Special Forces operatives could convince one small civilian female to get into a helicopter.

Matt's brain fed him a life-sized picture of that.

"We'd better get going," he said.

She looked up at him and a couple of snowflakes

caught in her lashes. They looked like stars sparkling in her eyes. She blinked and scrunched up her nose, and desire lanced through his groin, surprising the hell out of him.

Damn. At least it chased the drowsy haze from his head.

AIMEE FLEXED her right shoulder and suppressed a groan. It was already sore, and she had a feeling it would be black-and-blue by morning. She'd landed on it when the kidnapper tossed her out of the Hummer.

Matt glanced up as if he'd heard her. When she met his gaze, he gave her a little nod and then quickly looked back down at the small, handheld electronic device he held.

His effort to be reassuring wasn't very successful, though, mostly because he wasn't the kind of guy who could hide his feelings.

Throughout high school, college and the six years of Bill and Aimee's marriage, Bill and his three friends had been inseparable. They'd called themselves the Black Hills Brotherhood because of the near-death experience they'd shared as kids.

She knew all of them—Matt the best, because he'd been Bill's best friend.

It was interesting how alike the four were—and how different. Deke Cunningham and Rook Castle would have had no trouble winning at poker. Even Bill had always had a pretty good poker face.

Matt, on the other hand, was as easy to read as a first-grade storybook. Like right now. His brows drew down in a V across his forehead as he looked at the tiny screen of his device and then up at the cloudy sky.

He was worried about them reaching shelter before the storm hit. She was, too. It was getting dark, and the wind was picking up.

She wasn't sure why she'd asked about going back down the mountain. Maybe because it would have been nice to have a choice, even though she'd never leave without her child. Or maybe so she could understand exactly how bad things were, now that the Hummer had been destroyed.

They were on their own, with no transportation, a snowstorm on its way, and not one but two men who wanted to harm them. And her baby was still missing.

She figured she had a pretty good handle on how bad things were.

Per Matt's instructions, she'd dressed for the trip as if they were going to picnic at the North Pole. Layers, layers and more layers, he'd told her.

Of course, she'd lived in Wyoming all her life, so she knew how quickly the weather could change in the mountains, especially this time of year. And she knew that the most important thing to remember was to keep one's body core warm. So she had put on a tank top, silk long underwear, a cotton pullover, a wool sweater and her down jacket. She was set for any temperature.

Aimee's fingers were beginning to tingle with cold. She pulled off a mitten and stuffed her hand inside the elastic sleeve that covered her other arm. The skin-to-skin contact warmed her fingers almost instantly. The chill seeped into the skin of her other wrist, but it would warm back up within seconds.

She pulled her mitten back on and then did the same thing with her other hand.

Meanwhile, Matt was still studying the weather.

"Is everything okay?" she asked.

He stuck the handheld device into a pocket of the small daypack he carried on his back, and then smiled at her. "Sure. We need to get a move on, though. As I told you, it's going to take us an hour or so to get to the nearest shelter. And that storm is catching up to us."

She clenched her fists inside the mittens, and bit her cheek in an effort to stop the tears that stung her eyelids.

She'd been congratulating herself for already figuring all that out. Hearing Matt say it, however, seemed to make their situation more dire, and less simple. It was one thing for her to wonder if she were overstating their predicament. It was quite another to hear Matt verify that things really were that bad.

"Remind me again how everything is going to be all right?" she begged.

Matt tugged off his glove with his teeth and took it in his other hand. He stepped closer to her and touched her cheek, then her chin, with his warm fingers.

"Hey," he said, coaxing her chin upward so he could look into her eyes. "Pull your cap down. You look like you're getting cold."

"I'm a little chilly," she admitted. "Matt? How sure are you that William is okay?"

A shadow of doubt flickered across his face as he curled his lips in a smile. "Very sure. I promise you, we'll find him and he'll be fine."

As he spoke, the weight of worry that was squeezing her chest let up a little. It occurred to her that whatever he told her, she believed without reservation.

It was strange that his thoughtful answer coupled

with the uncertainty that had briefly touched his features, made him more believable than Bill, who had often stared at her expressionlessly, rather than giving her a straight answer.

She watched him closely. Was he more trustworthy than her husband had been? Or was Matt, too, trying to protect her from the truth?

His teeth scraped lightly across his lower lip as he checked his pack and got ready to go.

Aimee arched her shoulder again.

He'd said it would take about an hour to get to the shelter. She hoped he was being realistic, although she was afraid he was overestimating how fast she could move.

FOR THE NEXT HALF HOUR or so, Aimee kept up with Matt better than he would have expected. Not so much better that he revised his estimate of how long it would take them to get to the shelter, but fast enough to keep his body producing heat. From the sound of Aimee's breathing, she was keeping her heart rate up, too.

That was the good news. The bad news was that the storm was about to catch up to them. The wind was easterly, so it helped propel them forward, but the sun had gone down, the sky was cloudy and dark, and the air was heavy with moisture, making the wind bitingly cold.

They didn't talk much, just trudged along doggedly. Most of their conversation consisted of Matt asking if she was all right and Aimee replying that she was.

Then it started to snow, and Aimee started slowing down—way down.

He figured they were at least another half hour from the shelter. The temperature had dropped by at least ten degrees, he was sure, and the wind was probably up to thirty miles per hour, enough to make Aimee stumble when it gusted.

He wrapped an arm around her waist and half supported her, pushing her to walk a little faster. "Come on, Aimee. We're getting close. You've got to keep moving or you're going to get sick."

"I am a little chilly," she said, just as she had every time he'd asked.

Only this time, her words were slurred.

He reached back to a pocket of his daypack and retrieved a windup flashlight. He gave it about a minute's worth of winding. Then he shone it in her face.

"Wha—?" she said, her hand coming up to block the light.

"Stop for a second," he said. "I just want to take a look at your face."

"No. I'm fine." She kept going, one foot in front of the other, shuffling along. "I wanna get there."

"Aimee," he said more loudly. "Stop." He gripped her arm.

She tried to pull it out of his grasp, but it was a half-hearted effort. "No. Keep going," she muttered.

He shone the flashlight in her face, and saw how pale she was, and how translucent and gray her lips looked. He aimed the light at her eyes. How did the prettiest, plumpest snowflakes always manage to get caught in her lashes? They drifted away as she blinked against the flashlight's bright beam.

Her pupils were dilated, and barely reacted to the light.

It was what he'd been afraid would happen.

Aimee was hypothermic. If they didn't get to the shelter soon, she could die.

Chapter Six

Matt knew hypothermia didn't require freezing temperatures to affect someone. But he also knew they were being pummeled by winds that made the temperature that was already below freezing seem at least five degrees colder.

Plus the snow was wet, and dampness was seeping into their clothing.

He pulled off his down jacket, wrapped it around Aimee and snapped it closed. That gave her two layers of down, the best light insulation there was.

Then he dug the hood out of its pocket and tugged it down over her balaclava. He should have done that a long time ago, but he'd overestimated her endurance.

"Not a good idea," she muttered.

"What?"

"Now you'll be cold. We'll both be cold." She giggled faintly.

He was worried about her. "Come on, Aimee. We're not far from the shelter. Let's race."

"No," she drawled. "Don't wanna race. Tired."

"I know," he said, putting his arm around her again to support her and urge her on ahead.

"Sleepy, too. I need to get home. William's waiting for me."

"Aimee, do you know where we're going?"

For a moment, she didn't answer. Then, quietly, almost too quietly for him to hear, she spoke. "Home?"

He tightened his arm around her waist. "Listen, Aimee. We're up on Ragged Top Mountain. We're having an adventure. It's kind of like a treasure hunt." The wet snow was beginning to penetrate his wool sweater and underwear. He shivered, wishing he had the waterproof poncho that had burned up in his backpack.

"It's really important that we get to the shelter within the next twenty minutes. Can you walk really fast?"

She nodded. "I'm not sure. My feet aren't there." She laughed, a sound like ice cubes tinkling in a glass. "I mean, I know they're there. I just can't feel 'em."

"That's okay. They're there. I can see them." Matt smiled at her and looked up at the dark, cloud-filled sky. *God, help me get her to the shelter in time. Don't let me lose her. William needs her—I need her.*

MATT LIFTED THE BLANKETS that hung over the door to the shelter and pushed Aimee inside.

He'd already made her wait while he reconnoitered to be sure no one else was there. He figured both the kidnapper and Al Hamar already had a destination. The kidnapper was headed for wherever he was keeping the baby. And if Al Hamar had any sense he'd get off the mountain and get his wound attended to.

The shelter was primitive, with a wide opening on the east side and blankets as the only coverings for the two windows that faced north and south. The inside was ice-cold, but this version of ice-cold was at least ten degrees warmer than the outside. He shuddered as his body took note of the small increase in warmth.

After shrugging off the daypack, he shone the flashlight's beam around. Two cots, a fireplace, a couple of chairs. He examined every inch of the space.

Firewood? Where was firewood? Then he saw it. A small pile of limbs and branches against the far wall.

Under a window. Coated with a sheen of snow. What idiot had stored the firewood there? He grimaced. The wood was wet.

"Matt?" Aimee's voice quivered.

He pulled her toward one of the cots. "I've got to get you out of those wet clothes," he said firmly. "And get you under the covers. Hurry."

She looked at him without moving.

He pushed his jacket off her shoulders and jerked the insulated hood and watch cap off her head. Her hair was wet and she was shivering so much her teeth chattered.

"Okay, Aimee. We're going to get you warm. Trust me?"

"I'm a little chilly," she whispered.

"I know, sweetie, I know." He unzipped her down parka and pushed it down her arms. "I'm just going to get these wet things off you, okay?"

She nodded shakily. "I'm sleepy."

"That's good," he lied. His second lie to her.

Drowsiness was a symptom of hypothermia, a severe one. It meant her body temperature was dropping to dangerous levels. He had to work fast.

By the time he got the parka and her hiking boots off,

she'd almost quit shivering. That wasn't a good sign, either.

He talked to her while he undressed her. Nonsense things. Little reassurances, endearments, the kind of things one might use to soothe a frightened child.

Finally, she was down to a little tank top and her underpants. They weren't wet, but there wasn't enough to them to provide any warmth. All they were good for was preserving a little of her modesty and titillating him a lot.

Her skin was cool to the touch, and her fingers and toes were cold. He examined them closely, but they didn't appear to be frostbitten—yet.

He was tempted to rub them, but he knew better. Too much rubbing could damage freezing skin and nerves permanently.

He checked out the cots, which, thank God, weren't near the windows. The blanket he unfolded was slightly damp, but it was made of wool. Even wet, wool would still keep her warm—once he *got* her warm.

He lay her down on the cot and put the blanket over her.

"Stay there, okay? I need to get a fire going." He grabbed two blankets from the other cot and piled them over her, too.

Then he turned to the fireplace. The wood stacked inside it was wet, like all the other firewood. He brushed the snow away from the wood piled under the window and dug through it.

Toward the bottom, he found some sticks that weren't wet through. Grabbing an armful, he stacked them in the fireplace and took a couple of wet-weather fire-starter sticks out of his pack. He placed them under the branches and lit them with all-weather matches.

The starter sticks flared immediately. Now if the wood would just catch before they burned out. He adjusted a limb here, a branch there, until he was sure it was arranged for the best draft, and that was it. That was all he could do.

He watched for a few seconds, encouraged by the crackling and spitting as the hot flames generated by the starter sticks burned off the dampness.

He stripped down quickly, until he was covered in nothing but his boxers and goose bumps. All his clothes were wet, even his insulated underwear.

He was shivering, and he knew his body temp was down, but he wasn't hypothermic, thank God. His core was still warm.

Working as quickly as he could, and keeping one eye on the struggling fire and one on Aimee, he spread their clothes on chairs that he sat in front of the fireplace. If he could get the fire going, maybe they'd dry by morning.

He found some hurricane candles on a shelf and lit them, then carefully poked at the fire, checking the draft. To his relief, a few of the small branches caught.

"Hey, Aimee, I think we're going to have a fire before too long." He rose and picked up one of the hurricane candles. Crossing the room to the cot, he held it so the light shone on her face.

"Aimee, are you awake?" Her eyes were closed and she was lying too still. He touched her cheek, then reached under the blanket and found her hand. Icy. Dammit. He looked at her fingers. They were still white and pinched.

"Okay," he said, hoping his voice sounded calmer than he felt. "I'll tell you what we're going to do. I'm going to move the other cot next to the fire and lay you there. I've got a mummy bag—that's a head-to-toe sleeping bag, made for subzero conditions. It's a single, but if I unzip it, we can both get under it, like a blanket. How does that sound?"

He didn't like that she was nonresponsive. He knew how to treat hypothermia, but most recommended treatments assumed that dry clothes and a heat source were available.

Until the fire caught enough to actually generate heat, Matt only had one source of warmth available—his own body.

He checked the other cot. At least it was no wetter than the one Aimee was on. He pulled it over in front of the hearth, grabbed two of the blankets from on top of Aimee, and spread them over the mattress. The wool would hold the heat in.

Then he bent over Aimee. "Aimee, sweetie, can you wake up? I need you to wake up for me."

She stirred and opened her eyes. They were glassy and not quite focused. "Is it William?" she whispered.

His heart twisted. She was dreaming, maybe even hallucinating. "Aimee, listen to me. Sit up for me. Can you tell me how you feel?"

"I'm tired," she said. "Sleepy."

"I know. And you can go to sleep, just as soon as we get you over closer to the fire and get you warm. Come on. Let's move over to the fireplace."

She pushed at the blankets covering her.

"That's good. Here. I'm going to pull the covers down so you can get up."

Her eyes met his briefly. "Matt," she said. "What a nice surprise. Bill will be so glad you're here."

He'd thought he couldn't carry any more guilt, but her slurred words cut him to his soul. She *was* hallucinating. She thought Bill was still alive, thought they were all still friends.

Don't worry, he told himself. *Tomorrow she'll remember, and hate you again.*

If she lived until tomorrow. Unless he got her warm, she wouldn't last that long.

"Let's go," he said and lifted her to her feet. She almost collapsed against him. He wrapped his arm around her waist and half carried her to the cot.

Her skin felt cool, pressed against his. He had to get her body temp up—and fast. "Here we are," he said softly. "Just lie down there, and I'll get the sleeping bag."

She obeyed him without protest. She lay down and closed her eyes. "Cold," she murmured.

"I know, Aimee, but I'm going to fix that." He grabbed his daypack and retrieved the small bundle that was the compressed down sleeping bag. He pulled it out of its stuff-sack, unzipped it and shook it out to fluff the down.

"I'm just going to lay the sleeping bag over you, and then I'll put a couple of blankets on top."

He looked down at her. She lay on her side, facing the hearth, with her arms wrapped around her middle. The warm light from the fire made her pale skin look like the color of a ripe peach. Her bare legs and arms were silky and delicately muscled. The little top and panties emphasized her slender curves. Her dark hair was still damp and beginning to wave around her face.

She looked the way she had in high school. Fresh, beautiful, vibrant. No wonder Bill had fallen in love with her.

Matt swallowed against the lump that rose in his throat from just looking at her.

"All right, scumbag," he muttered to himself as he spread the down bag over her like a blanket. "Stop ogling and get started warming her up."

He fetched two more blankets. The down inside the sleeping bag was the ideal insulator. It was lightweight, held in heat and wicked out moisture. But Matt wanted some weight on top to seal in the heat his body produced, because he couldn't afford to lose even a couple of calories to the chilly room.

He carefully placed the blankets over the spread-out sleeping bag. Then, after a check of the fire to be sure it was lit and growing, he slid under the covers. Aimee's back was to him, so he cautiously moved closer. The scent of lemon assaulted his nostrils. How, after everything she'd been through, did she still smell so fresh and clean?

Her skin was cold, but apparently his body didn't care. When his groin came in contact with her backside, he swallowed a groan and grimaced. The feel of her supple body affected him—a *lot*.

He felt himself growing hard, felt his heart rate rise. Clenching his teeth and cursing himself for his weakness, he pulled away.

Aimee whimpered and scooted backward slightly.

Since her skin felt cool to him, his must feel hot to hers. "Okay, Aimee. I'm going to get as close to you as I can—" *and keep my sanity.* "It's just to warm you up. I promise I won't make you uncomfortable." Too bad he couldn't promise himself the same thing.

He scooted closer, wrapping his arm across her shoulders and pulling her close to his chest. He knew he had to concentrate on her core, rather than her chilled arms and legs. What made hypothermia deadly was that the body got chilled straight through. The most important thing was to warm up the vital organs. Once her core temperature rose, her arms and legs would start warming up.

He gritted his teeth and pressed his thighs against the backs of her legs.

Keep it professional, Parker.

After a while, Aimee's breathing grew more even, and she relaxed.

Matt lay there, listening to the wind and silently thanking whoever had built the shelter for taking the weather patterns up here into consideration. The shelter's solid back wall was turned against the predominant wind direction, which was easterly.

Aimee sighed in her sleep, and half turned, so that her cheek was no more than an inch from his nose. In the firelight he could see the faint dusting of freckles on her smooth skin. The scent of lemon and the delicate curve of her cheek made his mouth water.

He slid his hand down her arm, doing his best to avoid touching any other part of her. When he reached her wrist, he pressed his fingertips against the silky skin and counted her pulse. It was faint but steady. Then he took her hand in his.

At least her fingers weren't icy cold anymore. He sighed in relief. She was warming up. He was pretty sure she was out of danger. But he knew that if it had taken them any longer to get here, and if he hadn't been able to get a fire started, she could have died.

He breathed deeply and tried to relax. For the

moment, they were safe. He needed to get as much rest as he could while he had the chance.

Because tomorrow wasn't going to be easy. Tomorrow, he was going to have to explain to her why they were pressed up against each other and practically naked, why it made sense that he'd brought her up the mountain instead of down, and why he hadn't kept his promise to her—his promise to place William Matthew safely into her arms before the day was out.

Chapter Seven

Aimee came awake slowly. She was hot. And thirsty. She stirred, trying to push the covers back, but they wouldn't move. Someone was lying very close to her—too close. Someone with a very large, very warm body.

Her eyes flew open, and she saw the crackling fire.

Fire?

Where was she? Her pulse thrummed in her throat and she suddenly felt claustrophobic. She pushed herself up to a sitting position, kicking at the covers and gasping for breath.

"Aimee?"

"Who—?" She dug her heels in and propelled her body backward, away from whoever was pressing so close against her. She sucked in a huge breath, preparing to scream.

"Aimee, it's Matt."

A hand touched her shoulder.

She gasped and coughed.

"Shh. You're okay."

"Matt?" She blinked and looked at the figure that sat up next to her. "Matt? What are you doing—?"

She pushed at him.

"Aimee, whoa! You're going to fall off the cot."

He reached out toward her, but she recoiled instinctively. She was in bed—in bed! What kind of crazy dream was she having about Matt, of all people?

"I was just trying to warm you up. You were cold—too cold. I had to get your body temperature up. Do you remember?"

She stared at him, trying to process what he was saying. She couldn't, any more than she could figure out why she was here in this strange room next to him.

He was bare-chested, his skin glowing like gold in the firelight. His dark hair was tousled and wavy, as if he'd just toweled it dry.

She lifted the edge of the covers and looked down at herself. All she had on was a little tank top and panties.

"What's going on? Why—?" Had Matt undressed her? She raised her shocked gaze to his and absently registered a look of apology in his expression.

"I had to," he said. "You were freezing."

She stared at him as bits of memories flashed across her brain.

Matt wrapping an arm around her and telling her she was going to be okay.

Snow blowing in her face, her eyes and lips stinging with cold—the smell of gasoline—the sounds of gunfire—

And the awful, menacing words crackling down the phone wire. "If you want to see your baby again, *you* will deliver the money."

If you want to see your baby again—

"William!" she cried, his name ripping from her throat. Suddenly they were all there. All the memories. All the terror. All the anguish. "My baby! Where is he?"

"Aimee, shh. Try to stay calm."

She heard the words, but hardly registered where they came from. All she knew was that they cut like a razor through her heart.

"Calm? My baby is gone. They stole him, out of his bed." Her hands flew to her mouth. "I was asleep. I was asleep and they took him."

Her eyes burned, and her mouth was dry. So dry. She licked her lips.

"You're thirsty. I'll get you some water."

It was Matt, she realized. Bill's best friend.

Safe as houses.

But he wasn't. He'd taken Bill away from her and let him die. He'd shown up like a knight in shining armor at the very moment when she needed a hero, but he'd let William's kidnapper get away, and he didn't save her baby. Pain lanced through her and she clutched at her middle.

When Matt rose, she saw that his lower body was almost as bare as his upper. He was dressed in nothing but snug-fitting boxers.

They *both* were nearly naked. She rubbed her temple, wishing she could put all this information together and come up with a reasonable understanding of what was happening.

She knew who he was now. And she knew they hadn't rescued William. But where were they? And how had they gotten there?

"I melted some snow, once the fire got going," he said conversationally. He picked up a metal cup and filled it from a pan that sat near the fireplace.

"Here." He held out the cup.

She couldn't move. She still clutched the covers to her chest like a shield.

"Come on, Aimee. Take the cup. You need to drink some water." Slowly, carefully, he reached out a hand and took hers, gently prying her fingers loose from the blanket, and pressed the cup into her palm. It was cool.

He turned and went back to the fire, where he picked up pieces of clothing. For the first time she noticed two straight-backed chairs by the hearth.

He piled the clothes on the hearth and spread other pieces over the backs of the chairs.

She watched him as she lifted the cup to her lips. The flat, tepid water tasted wonderful. She drank the whole cupful.

"Our clothes will probably be dry by morning."

"Could I have some more?" she asked, and at once felt guilty because she was warm and safe and enjoying water while her baby was out there somewhere— alone. Maybe thirsty. Maybe cold. The pain hit her again, swift and sharp.

"Oh—" she gasped.

Matt took the cup from her hands. "What's wrong? Are you hurting?"

"I want—I need my baby." Tears stung her eyes, but she lifted her chin and swallowed them. "Do you—" She paused, terribly afraid she knew the answer to the question she was about to ask. "Do you know where he is?"

He filled the cup and handed it back to her, then filled another one and drank it himself. He went back to checking and rearranging the clothing. "No. I don't know where he is right now. But the storm is almost over and I'm hoping that by morning the clouds will have cleared away. We'll meet Deke at the rendezvous point and he can take you back with him. As soon as I find William, I'll—"

"What?" She was still having trouble sorting everything out, but her brain finally put his words together in the proper order.

He can take you back with him.

"No!" She slammed the cup down on the wooden floor with a clang. "I am not going back without my baby."

"Aimee, you have to. You can't stay up here. I don't have the supplies or shelter to take care of you."

"Why can't Deke bring supplies?"

"Because he's going to get you to get you to safety while I rescue William." He picked up a pair of dark leggings, pulled them up and tugged a matching long-sleeved shirt over his head.

"But—"

"Listen to me, Aimee. I can't concentrate on rescuing William if I'm worried about you." He sorted through the clothes until he found her silk turtleneck and handed it to her.

"You need to put this on and get back under the covers. It's still a couple of hours until morning. After the snowstorm started, you got hypothermic. So from now on you're going to be susceptible to the cold. You need all the strength you can muster."

She took the shirt and pulled it on. "Don't ignore me,

Matt. And don't treat me like I'm going to break. I was confused when I first woke up, but I'm not now." *Not completely.*

She smoothed the shirt down over her abdomen. "I can't sleep anymore. William is out there. I have to get ready. We have to go find him."

Matt sat on his haunches, tossed back the rest of his water and sat the cup on the hearth. He picked up a stick and poked the fire.

"You need to rest," he said again, not looking at her.

She wanted to be angry at him, needed to be. But his quiet, deliberate actions didn't invite attacks. In fact, his composure was calming.

For a moment she was mesmerized by the silhouette of his profile, outlined by the orange glow from the coals. It was classic and grim. She could believe he was an ancient warrior, staring into the flames as he prepared his mind for battle.

Suddenly, a memory from the night before flashed across her mind. He'd been lying next to her on the cot, his legs and chest pressed against her from behind. She remembered the thick warmth of his skin against hers, the rapid rise and fall of his chest and belly. The feel of his erection, hard and hot against her. He'd groaned, then whispered something.

I promise.

That was all she remembered. But she knew that, whatever that promise had been, he'd keep it.

It occurred to her that he was in his element here. Weather and survival had been his specialties in the Air Force. There were probably only a handful of people in the world as well trained as Matt to rescue her baby.

He hadn't been exaggerating when he said he couldn't take care of her and do his job. She was definitely a handicap. She knew that. He couldn't move as fast or as stealthily with her along. He couldn't focus all his concentration and energy on overpowering the kidnapper and rescuing William if he had to be concerned about her safety. But she was right, too. When he found William, she had to be there.

Matt might be the only person she could trust to find her child, but she was the only one who could protect him.

BY THE TIME they got away from the shelter, it was after 0700 hours. Matt had figured out hours earlier that they were going to miss the 0800 rendezvous point he'd arranged with Deke. To have any chance of making it, they'd have had to leave before daylight, while the wet snow was still falling. And he wasn't about to expose Aimee to the possibility of hypothermia again.

He'd ventured out of the shelter several times during the night to check the weather. The storm had done exactly what he'd figured it would do. It had moved in ahead of predictions. But what he hadn't expected was the second front that had moved in right behind it. He'd seen the low pressure system that had been building behind the first. It hadn't looked significant, and it had been hours behind the first, larger storm.

But then the first storm had stalled, hovering over the mountain for hours after its predicted movement eastward. The extra time gave the second storm plenty of time to catch up and gain strength.

Yesterday's weather forecast had the second storm not moving in for another twelve hours. However, by the time the first storm passed through, the second one was already rolling in.

The good news was that it was a weaker front, and hadn't dropped nearly as much snow. By 0630 the snow had stopped and the storm was beginning to dissipate.

Matt figured that within another hour the skies might be clear enough for him to use his satellite phone.

He'd found a pair of snowshoes in the shelter. He gave them to Aimee, despite her protests. He could survive, even if his feet got wet. She couldn't.

In the place of the snowshoes, the firewood, a liter-sized plastic bottle filled with melted snow, and two of the wool blankets, Matt had left four of his eight remaining fire-starter sticks and extra all-weather matches for the next traveler who sought refuge there.

He'd fashioned one of the blankets into a makeshift pack, tying the corners into knots and using duct tape from his daypack. So this morning he carried the makeshift pack containing his electronic devices, the water, the other blanket, several high-calorie protein bars, and the money, and Aimee carried the daypack with the sleeping bag and the lighter items. He had the heavy machine pistol and she had the Glock.

"Let's go, Aimee," he called. He'd told her to stay in the shelter until he was sure they were ready to go.

She appeared at the opening, stuffing strands of hair inside the balaclava she'd folded up and donned like a ski cap. Her face was rosy and fresh-looking. Thank God her pallor from the night before was gone.

"You walk in front."

"Are you sure?" she asked. "Wouldn't it be better if you set the pace?"

He looked at her in surprise. "That's a good question."

"You don't have to act like you're about to faint. I told you, I've done a little hiking in my time."

"Letting me set the pace would be a good idea, if we were evenly matched. But you wouldn't be able to keep up with me. If I lead, I'll be tempted to walk too fast, and then I'll have to slow down to let you catch up. That'll be extremely tiring for me. At the same time, you'll be trying to keep pace when I speed up, which will make *you* very tired. If you set the pace, you can adjust it to your level of conditioning, and I can find your rhythm. That way we'll both conserve our energy."

Aimee sent him a little smile. "All that *and* good-looking."

His brows rose. She'd surprised him again.

"Yeah," he replied. It was good to see her smile. He suspected it was unlikely that she was genuinely amused. She was probably just putting on a front, hoping he wouldn't figure out how scared she was.

As if he could miss it.

She moved in front of him, a little uncertain balancing on the snowshoes.

After the third time she almost stumbled, he called out, "I thought you'd done some hiking."

"I didn't say it was in snow."

He smiled again, and a warmth that had nothing to do with the temperature spread through him. "Now you tell me."

He looked at his watch. By his best calculations, they were about six miles away from where Deke would be circling, looking for them.

Judging by the time they'd made last night, allowing for the fact that they weren't battling a snowstorm and Aimee wasn't handicapped by hypothermia this morning, it would still take them at least two hours, maybe more, to get there, trudging through the wet, packed snow. He figured the temperature was about thirty degrees.

And it would rise as the sun rose. While that meant they'd spend the day peeling off layers of clothing so they wouldn't sweat, at least the heat would burn off the rest of the clouds.

Aimee said something that the wind picked up and blew away.

"What?" he called out.

She turned her head. "Do the clouds look like they're thinning? Can you get a signal on your phone?"

He looked up at the clouds that hung heavily above them. They were dissipating behind them, to the west. Pulling out the satellite phone, he checked the signal.

Nothing.

"Not yet."

He kept checking over the next hour. Finally, the phone responded with a weak signal. He dialed Irina.

"Matt!" she cried as soon as she picked up the phone. "What happened? Where are you? Do you have the baby?"

"No. But the kidnapper doesn't have the money, either. We're headed toward the first rendezvous point, but we're not going to make it in time. Tell Deke we can be there by 1000 hours for sure—"

"Matt, listen. The helicopter's been sabotaged."

Had he heard right? "Sabotaged? There at the ranch with all your security? That's impossible!"

"It happened. We don't know how. Someone drained all the oil. When Deke tried to take off, the motor burned up. It's going to take all day to put in a new motor."

"Deke would never take off without checking everything."

"Right. The oil gauge registered full. It had been tampered with."

"What can he do? I need to get Aimee out of here. She's not trained for this weather or this terrain, and most of my supplies burned up in the Hummer."

"Repeat. I missed that."

"My supplies burned up in the Hummer."

"The Hummer burned? You're on foot?"

"Yeah."

"—get Deke right on it. But listen. There's something—at least two more—"

"You're breaking up."

"More storms—this way."

"Okay. I'll check it out."

"There's one blowing in now. It'll probably reach—area—Ragged Top within the next two hours."

"Damn," Matt breathed. "Okay. I can deal with the weather. What else?"

"It's big, Matt. Schiff got an anonymous call early this morning. The caller said—Aimee's ba—the Vick cabin—get that?"

"Baby? Cabin?" Matt looked at Aimee. She'd been listening to his side of the conversation the whole time. She met his gaze. He knew shock and relief were plastered all over his face.

Her face lit up, tempered with hesitancy, as if she

weren't quite sure she should actually dare to be excited yet.

He nodded at her and smiled. "Got it."

"—gave him the kidna—"

"Gave him what?"

"Name. It's Kinnard."

"Kinnard?"

"The police are familiar with him. He's a small-time hood—muscle for some local loan sharks, that sort of thing. And years ago—arently did work for Boss—"

"For who?"

"Boss Vick."

That shocked Matt. He turned away from Aimee's curious gaze. For the moment, it might be wise to keep that last tidbit of information to himself.

"Can you verify that?"

"Margo denies ever hearing—less knowing him—warrant for—papers. But—to take—"

"Irina, I can barely understand you. Can Deke make the Sunday rendezvous?"

"—get in—pick up—Sunday 0900."

"Got it, 0900. Out."

Matt disconnected, and then tried to access the weather reports via satellite. But the cloud cover was getting thicker, and reception was spotty.

He'd have to continue to rely on old-fashioned methods of reading the weather and predicting what would happen next.

"Matt?" Aimee had waited patiently while he talked to Irina, but he could see that she was bursting with curiosity. "Did she say *baby?* At the cabin?" she asked hesitantly.

"Someone called in an anonymous tip this morning, letting the FBI know that your baby, your William, is there."

"He's there? At the cabin? Oh—" Aimee capped a hand over her mouth. Her eyes glittered with unshed tears. "Oh, Matt. Do you think the caller was telling the truth? Do you really think he's all right?"

Matt nodded. "From what Irina said, it sounds like he's fine."

She pressed her fingertips to her lips for a few seconds, then ran toward him.

Before he realized what she was doing, she slammed into him, wrapping her arms around his neck and hugging him tighter than he'd ever been hugged in his life.

He stood there for a second, not knowing how to react. But her joy, her relief, her sheer happiness at knowing her child was safe, began to seep in past his reserve. He wrapped his arms around her and hugged her back.

She buried her face in the hollow between his neck and shoulder and hung on. After a few seconds, he realized that he felt tears against his neck.

"Hey," he said, gently pushing her away and peering at her. "Are you okay?"

She nodded as tears flowed down her cheeks and ran over the corner of her mouth. She sniffed. "I'm so—so relieved. I was so scared."

His heart was twisting again. He'd never known an internal organ could warp in so many different directions. "I know you were. I don't think I've ever seen you cry."

She swiped her fingers across her cheeks. "I don't. Ever."

"I guess this is a pretty special occasion then."

Her smile broadened and she laughed. "I guess it is." She blew air out between her lips, wiped her cheeks again, and then straightened and looked him in the eye.

"So how far are we from the cabin? How fast can we get there? Who's there with him?"

"Whoa," Matt said, holding up his hands. "I can't tell you who's there with him, but I can tell you that we're about ten miles from the cabin and we can get there in four or five hours. But only if you turn around and walk."

She grinned at him. "Which direction?"

The maps he'd memorized suddenly went completely out of his head, knocked out by the dazzle of her grin. He'd seen it before, of course, but not in a long time. And never directed solely at him.

"Hang on a minute," he croaked, holding up a hand. He pulled his glove off with his teeth and retrieved the printed maps from his pocket. After a little shuffling, he came up with the right one.

"Okay. Bear 18 degrees north of east."

"Bear what?"

He laughed ruefully, held up the compass and took the reading, then pointed. "Go thataway."

She turned and looked. "Thataway?"

He shook his head. "Walk!"

With a swish of her hips, the impact of which was mostly lost under the down parka, Aimee turned and started walking.

Matt stuffed his maps back into his pocket and tugged on his glove, all the while lecturing himself about how uncool it was to be lusting after his best friend's widow.

Especially here. Especially now. They were in a dangerous situation. His job was to take care of her, to protect her. Getting emotional led to screwups. He knew that from personal experience.

Twenty years ago, he, Deke, Rook and Bill had found themselves trapped on a mountain ledge when a storm blew in. He'd been the youngest of the four, and the most scared. Rook and Deke, and even Bill, only two months older than him, had stayed calm. But he'd sobbed as the reclusive Vietnam vet Arlis Hanks had pulled him up using a rope and a block and tackle. That was the last time he'd cried.

Shaking his head at the memory, Matt looked up.

Aimee was nowhere in sight.

Chapter Eight

"Aimee!" Matt shouted. "Aimee!" His heart slammed against his chest wall, ripping the breath from his lungs.

He broke into a run. The terrain here was fairly even, and the trees were sparse. He could see for several yards. How could she have disappeared?

God, please don't let her have fallen over a ledge.

That thought stopped him in his tracks as alarm sheared his breath.

Stay calm. Cool. Rational.

The words echoed in his head with each cautious step he took. Combined with deep, even breaths, they helped to slow his pounding heart. He placed his feet into her snowshoe prints.

Within about ten paces he saw the indented ribbon of snow that marked a creek bed. She must have fallen in.

"Aimee!" he shouted.

"Matt! Here!" Her voice was shrill with fear.

"Stay still. I'll be right there." Within a few steps, he could see the hole in the snow. He approached carefully.

Several feet from the place where Aimee had fallen, he lowered himself to his hands and knees and crawled until he could peer over the edge.

Aimee was sitting in a pile of snow.

"Aimee? Don't move. Are you all right?"

She looked up. "Yes," she said disgustedly. "My butt hurts, but not as much as my pride." She moved to stand.

"Wait. Are you sure you're okay? Nothing's sprained? Wrists? Ankles?"

She shook her head. "I've checked everything. I didn't move because I didn't know how I was going to get back up there."

Matt laughed. "That's easy," he said, and proceeded to show her just how easy it was.

Back on high ground and standing beside Matt, Aimee brushed snow off her pants as she surveyed the place where she'd fallen. "What did I fall into?"

"A creek bed, and not even a very deep one." He pointed behind them and then in front, tracing the creek's meandering path to where it disappeared among the evergreen trees. "See that narrow ribbon of snow that's kind of sunken?"

"Oh. I should have seen that." It would have saved her a sore butt and sore pride. "So all that extra snow blew into the creek? It sort of collects it, I guess."

"That's exactly right. Spend much time hiking in the snow and you learn to notice things you might not otherwise. Little signs like that dip in the snow or a shadow that might indicate a rock. Things that can hurt you or even kill you if you don't pay attention."

"Okay, so tell me again why I'm leading, if you're the expert?" She grinned at him. Not even her fall could spoil her good mood. She felt like laughing and running and dancing.

In a little while, she would have her baby back in her arms, safe and sound. That was worth every minute of the past day. Every second.

Matt's brows drew down. "Good point," he said. "Okay. I'll take the lead, but you've got to keep up. Tell me if I go too fast."

"Okay, sir," she said. "You go in front, sir, and I'll follow. But please, keep showing me the secrets the snow is covering up. Never know when that kind of thing might come in handy."

Before they headed out again, Matt shed his parka and stuffed it inside his makeshift pack.

The snug-fitting wool sweater he wore over his insulated underwear glistened in the sunlight. Wool was too fuzzy to clearly outline the muscles in his arms and torso, but Aimee hadn't forgotten how he looked with the firelight glinting off the planes and angles of his naked torso last night. Nor had she forgotten how his warm, strong body felt pressed against her.

Bill had been good-looking, with his light brown hair, his hazel eyes and the dimples all the girls in high school had gone crazy over. He was always voted most handsome and most likely to succeed. He'd been big and tall, and captain of the football team.

Matt, on the other hand, had once been voted most shy. His dark hair, brown eyes and strong features weren't as classically handsome as Bill's had been. His nose was a little too long, and he'd never played football. He'd been on the swim team. His muscles had always been long and lean. In fact, some had considered him downright scrawny.

But after last night, Aimee had decided that Matt was a dangerously attractive and sexy man.

"Okay, let's go," he said, sending her a puzzled look. "You sure you're okay?"

She nodded and shrugged her shoulders to rearrange the daypack into a comfortable position. As she moved into step behind him, she considered her thoughts.

She was sure she'd seen him in a bathing suit. She was positive she had. She and Bill and Matt had all gone down to Florida on spring break one year, and they'd all stayed in the same room. But she hardly remembered Matt at all. What she remembered about that trip was that she and Bill had had sex for the first time. In the hotel room—with Matt asleep on the other bed.

Her cheeks burned. Dear heavens, what had she been thinking? Granted, it was years ago, probably long forgotten by Matt, if he'd even woken up, but still—how embarrassing.

And now, after having spent the night pressed against his lean, hard body, thinking about that long-ago experience kind of turned her on. Guilt brought heat to her cold cheeks.

Stop it, she warned herself.

Matt held up a hand. "Shh."

She froze.

He sent her a quick look over his shoulder, and then cocked his head, listening.

Before she realized that he'd moved, Matt had grabbed her arm and pulled her toward him. He propelled her over to a stand of trees and followed her several feet in, until they were surrounded by trees on all sides.

Then he crouched down, and pulled her back between his knees.

"Stay quiet," he whispered in her ear.

"What is—"

He put his fingers across her mouth. She nodded against them and after a couple of seconds, he removed them.

For a long time, they crouched there, spooned awkwardly. Even through layers of clothes, the sense of intimacy was as strong as it had been the night before.

Her insides stirred, tingling with sensations that she hadn't felt in a long time. She yearned to lean back, to press herself against Matt the way he'd pressed his body against hers last night. Her eyes drifted closed as the tingling centered itself in her core.

He put his hands on her shoulders. She wanted to cover them with hers, to take them and pull them around her, so she could feel the way she'd felt last night. As much as it scared her to admit that she wanted him, that was how much she longed for him to touch her, to kiss her and, yes, to make love with her.

She told herself it was because he made her feel safe.

His fingers squeezed her shoulders, massaging them. He leaned forward, his breath warming her cheek. Was he feeling the same thing she was?

Then she heard it. A buzzing sound. Very faint. She turned her head but she couldn't tell where it was coming from. What was it? An engine?

Her pulse sped up. An engine. A helicopter! Maybe it was Deke, coming to rescue them. He could take them to the Vicks' cabin and help them rescue William. Her breath caught in an excited sob.

But if it were Deke's helicopter, why were they hiding?

"Is that an engine?" she whispered.

Matt put his ear next to hers and nodded his head.

"Helicopter?" she asked hopefully.

He shook his head no. "Snowmobile."

Snowmobile? But that could be anybody.

Anybody.

"Oh."

He pressed his fingertips against her lips again, warning her to stay quiet.

Slowly, over what seemed to be an endless stretch of time, the noise of the engine grew louder. It kept growing louder, until it sounded like it was close enough to run them down.

Matt put his hand on the back of her head. "Put your head down. And don't move."

As she lowered her head, Matt pressed his forehead against her back. She could imagine what the two of them looked like. Two small, fragile humans dwarfed by the tall trees, crouched together, hoping and praying that they couldn't be seen by someone whizzing by on a snowmobile. Or someone searching for them—

Her heart pounded so loud she was afraid it could be heard over the motor's noise.

As the engine noise grew deafening, she felt Matt straighten. He left his hand resting gently on the back of her neck, so she didn't budge. He grew so still that if it weren't for the slow, steady rise and fall of his chest, she might have been able to forget he was there, pressed against her.

Okay, no. She wouldn't forget the feeling of his body molded to hers—not for a very long time.

Finally, the noise of the engine faded into the distance. Aimee waited until Matt took his hand away from the nape of her neck before she sat up.

"Ah," she moaned as her muscles relaxed from their cramped position. She looked at Matt. "Who was it? Could you see anything?"

He nodded grimly.

"Was it the kidnapper?"

"Nope. It was Al Hamar. There was a lot of blood on his pants. The kidnapper must have hit him in the side. He didn't look happy, but he didn't look like he was too handicapped by the wound, either."

"He didn't see us." She phrased it as a statement, but she watched Matt's face for confirmation. "Where do you think he's going?"

He rubbed his thumb across his lower lip, and averted his gaze. "I'm afraid he's probably headed for the cabin, just as we are."

And as quickly as that, all sense of safety, all confidence, all joy at the knowledge that William was only a few miles away and safe, dissolved, and Aimee was back in that awful place where she'd existed since six-thirty Wednesday morning.

"Why?" she moaned. "I thought you didn't think he was connected with the kidnapping. How would he know about the cabin?"

Matt's jaw clenched. After an instant of wavering, his gaze met hers. "All I can figure out is that both he and Kinnard are—"

"Kinnard?" Aimee didn't like how Matt was acting. He obviously didn't want to tell her something.

"That's the kidnapper's name."

"The man who took William? Who is he?"

"According to the FBI, he's a small-time hood who has operated around the Crook County area for the past twenty years or so."

"You said *apparently.*"

Matt straightened. "We should get going."

"No. *You* should tell me what's going on. Who do you think Kinnard is, and what are you trying not to tell me?"

"I think both men are working for Novus Ordo."

"Novus Ordo? The terrorist?" She felt the blood drain from her face. She'd thought nothing could be as bad as having her baby kidnapped. But by *terrorists?*

"You're talking about Novus Ordo?" she asked. "The man whose face nobody has ever seen? The one they say is more dangerous than Bin Laden?"

Matt swallowed and reluctantly met her gaze. "We believe he had Rook Castle assassinated, because Rook saw him—he may be the only person outside Novus's inner circle who has ever seen the man's face."

"I don't—understand." What did Rook Castle and an infamous terrorist have to do with her? With her baby?

"I know. It's complicated. But the theory is that since Rook's body was never recovered, and since Irina has been searching for him all this time, Novus has been watching her, just in case."

"In case Rook is still alive." Aimee couldn't believe she was hearing—much less beginning to understand— what Matt was saying.

Matt nodded. "So since security is so tight around Castle Ranch that Irina and Deke are virtually untouchable, Novus is trying to capture me, to interrogate me about Rook."

"So a *terrorist* kidnapped *my baby* to get to you?"

"I'm not positive, but if Kinnard is working for Novus, and if the anonymous caller was telling the truth—"

"Then the cabin is a trap." Aimee's heart felt ripped to shreds. She put her gloved hands to her mouth and breathed into them, trying to stop the panic from rising in her throat. She spoke, her words muffled by the thick gloves.

"We can't go to the cabin." She swallowed panic and fear and breathed in courage. "They'll capture you."

Matt took her hands away from her mouth and held them. "I made you a promise. Nothing—*nothing*—is going to stop me from keeping it."

Her breath hitched.

"Everything we know points to William being at the cabin. We're going."

SATURDAY 1400 HOURS

"REMEMBER WHAT I TOLD YOU," Matt said.

Aimee barely heard him. It had taken four hours, but they were finally looking down at the cabin from their vantage point on a rise to the west.

She stared at the primitive log structure. She knew a little about it from Bill. His father, Boss Vick, had spent an obscene amount of money to equip the simple dwelling.

He'd brought a crew up one summer who'd cleared trees, installed a generator and carted appliances and furniture up. He'd made it into a comfortable winter retreat, if one didn't mind skiing in or living with the prospect of being snowed in.

Aimee had always thought the idea of spending so

much on a hunting shack was wasteful, but right now, the amenities sounded wonderful to her—the generator, the appliances, the comfortable furnishings—because they meant that her baby was warm and comfortable and well-fed.

And in the hands of terrorists.

"Aimee? Did you hear me?"

She nodded. "I don't make a move until you've gone down there and verified that nobody is waiting to shoot us when we step out into the open." She couldn't take her eyes off the house. She squinted, but couldn't see through any of the windows. But that was okay. Whether she could see him or not, her baby was in there. Her fingers itched—her arms ached—to hold him.

But Matt was right. They had to take precautions. There were at least two people on this mountain who meant them harm.

"You'll wave *all clear,* and motion me to come down. Or you'll hold up your hands, palms out, and press them down, meaning stay where I am." She demonstrated what he'd shown her earlier.

"Good. And if something happens to me?"

She pressed her lips together and squeezed her eyes shut. "I run for the cabin. Matt, maybe this is not a good idea. Maybe we ought to wait until Deke gets here. Spend the night up here, or—"

It nearly killed her to suggest waiting. She thought she was going to die if she had to wait one second longer to hold her baby, but the prospect of Matt being captured by terrorists—captured and interrogated—was nearly as horrible to contemplate as the possibility that she might never see William again.

"No." He shook his head, dislodging snowflakes from his hair. He held out his gloved hand and several more fell onto it. "See that? It's starting to snow again. The storms from last night are only the beginning. There are more stacked up, waiting for their shot at us. And we have no shelter." He craned his neck and examined the sky.

"There's a very good chance that we wouldn't survive the night. With just the mummy bag for the two of us, it's too risky. Getting to the cabin is our best chance."

"What if we both go down at the same time? We can watch each other's backs. You'll have that machine gun thing and I have the Glock. We can hold them off."

His face softened into an almost-smile. "Or…we could wait until nightfall. We could probably sit out a storm during the day without freezing to death. Even behind the clouds, the sun still provides a lot of heat. But after sundown is a different story."

"I like that idea—waiting until dark."

Matt kept his gaze on the cabin and the surrounding area. "We need to get to work if we're going to spend the rest of the day here. I want to build a snow shelter. It'll hide us and keep us warm after the clouds roll in. Plus it'll protect us from the snow and the wind." He peered through the trees at the cabin, then scanned the tree line above and below the clearing. He didn't see anyone.

That didn't surprise him. Kinnard was definitely right at home on the mountain, and Al Hamar was almost certainly from a mountainous country—Afghanistan or Pakistan—and trained in guerrilla tactics. Either one of them could be anywhere—in the cabin or hiding out, ready to ambush Matt and Aimee as they approached it.

"We don't want to be seen, so we have to work quickly and at the same time stay hidden. So be prepared to crawl around."

"What do you need me to do?"

"Right now, keep an eye on the cabin while I scout around for the best place to locate our shelter. I like that overhanging rock over there. We need to hurry, though. From the looks of the sky, by the time we get the shelter built, we're going to be very glad to have it."

SURE ENOUGH, by the time the shelter was ready, the new storm had rolled in, bringing another sky full of heavy, snow-laden clouds and a nasty mix of freezing rain and snow.

Aimee sat inside the cramped space, waiting for Matt to come inside. He'd spread a space blanket on the ground and folded one of the blankets on top of it. He'd covered the downhill side of the lean-to with the other blanket, and that made a huge difference in the inside temperature.

Matt pushed aside the blanket and climbed inside, bringing freezing air and icy spray with him. He'd taken off his parka, which he draped over the make-shift backpack. "Not bad, if I do say so myself. What do you think?"

She tried to smile, but she knew she wasn't pulling it off. "Better than the Ritz."

"Hey," he said, his voice closer than she'd expected. It was nearly pitch-black with the blanket closed. And granted, the entire space of the shelter was about six feet by three feet. Still, she'd figured he'd hover near one side and she'd cling to the other.

"How're you doing? It'll be dark within about three hours. Then we can sneak down to the cabin and check things out. Meanwhile…" He paused and took a breath. "Meanwhile, you should take off your parka. Believe it or not, it'll be easier to adjust to the temperature without it on. Plus, when we get ready to go, you'll be glad you have another layer to put on."

Aimee carefully shrugged out of the down jacket. She held on to it and used it to cover her hands. She'd taken off her gloves, which were wet from piling and packing snow.

"Matt, can I ask you a question?"

"Sure. Anything."

"You said Irina and Deke were untouchable because of the security around the ranch."

"Right. Rook installed the best equipment money could buy. And all the employees are screened carefully."

"But when you were talking to Irina, you mentioned sabotage. At the ranch."

He stared at her for a moment. "I did. Somebody tampered with Deke's helicopter. Irina said it was definitely sabotage." He cursed. "I heard it but it didn't sink in. Irina could be in danger." He shook his head.

"You're awfully hard on yourself."

"What?"

Aimee sent him a small smile. "You're out here, protecting me, and doing your best to rescue my baby, but at the same time you're beating yourself up for not thinking about Irina's possible danger."

He shrugged. "I feel responsible."

"I know you do. It's the kind of man you are." She settled against the rock that formed the back of their

lean-to. "From everything I know about Deke Cunningham, I'm guessing he can protect Irina."

"Yeah. He can."

For several minutes, they sat silently. Aimee could
feel Matt's tension. Was he still kicking himself? She
figured it was time to change the subject.

She looked around at the shelter he'd built. "I guess this
is how the first Americans lived for hundreds of years."

"Thousands. Yeah. We're soft these days."

"Not you," she said, poking his bicep with her finger.

He laughed, a soft rumbling sound. "Yeah, me."

She lay her hand on his arm. "Not you," she murmured.

His gaze snapped to hers. Even in the near blackness,
his dark eyes picked up a reflection from somewhere.
And in that reflection was the thing that had been born
of their necessary closeness in the shelter the night
before. The awareness that they were not just two people
bound by their love for his friend and her husband.

Aimee cringed at what she'd done. One poke might
have been just an innocent gesture. One teasing touch
could be ascribed to friendship. But she'd touched him
twice. She'd *lingered.*

That was no innocent gesture.

After the awkward silence had swelled to uncomfortable proportions, he uttered a small chuckle. "Oh? Well,
what about you? You aren't looking so bad." He slid his
hand along the line of her shoulder and upper arm. "A
little on this side of skinny."

That was all. Yet her body burned as if he'd trailed
hot fingers over its entire length.

"My guess is you've got some fair-sized biceps
yourself."

Aimee moistened her lips.

Innocent teasing, she told herself. That's all it was. How long had it been since she'd felt like laughing, even a little bit? Other than when she played with William. Besides, she'd known Matt for most of her life. He was a friend.

There might be a smidgen of sexual tension between them, the natural attraction between a man and a woman forced together by circumstance. That's all this was.

Natural. Understandable. Easily ignored.

What could a little teasing hurt? It was better than sitting here in gloomy silence for hours. A little humor would help pass the time.

She squeezed her fist and flexed her arm muscles. "Fair-sized biceps? I beg your pardon. Check this out."

His fingers closed around her biceps—it felt like they completely circled her upper arm.

"Yeah," he said softly. "You're a regular American Gladiator."

His breath fanned her cheek. He was that close.

Aimee had no idea what to do next. However, apparently he did. He let go of her arm and slid his hand around her shoulders.

"Here." His voice rumbled through her like the purr of a lion. "We can keep each other warm."

His arm was firm and big and comforting, and his body radiated heat. Aimee was tempted to tuck herself into the warm, safe nook created by his torso and arm.

He pulled her closer.

She sighed and gave in to temptation, relaxing against him.

His breaths ruffled her hair. She raised her head,

wanting to feel him breathing on her skin. When she did, her nose brushed his chin, and she breathed in his scent. He smelled of snow and evergreen, with a hint of smokiness. It plummeted her back to the night before and his warm embrace.

Her breath caught.

He uttered a small moan, deep in his throat, and then pressed his forehead against hers and slid his fingers up her shoulder to cradle the back of her head.

"Aimee—"

Her heart fluttered—with fear or desire, she wasn't sure. She had no idea what he was going to do or say. She had no idea what she *wanted* him to do or say. As far as she was concerned, they could sit like this for the next three hours.

She was pretty sure that three hours of Matt's full attention would bolster not only her courage, but her energy and her resolve, as well.

"Aimee, I need to tell you something."

She rolled her forehead from side to side against his. "No, you don't." *Don't ruin this moment with reality. Don't make it anything more than it is. A stolen instant out of time.*

"I do. I need to expl—"

She kissed him. Just grabbed his face between her hands and—smack. No hesitation, no nips or teases or nibbles. Just a full-on, openmouthed kiss.

And she did it because sitting here in this dangerous, tense situation, pursued by men who could be working for the most ruthless terrorist on the planet, waiting for nightfall so they could rescue her seven-month-old baby, she still felt safer than she had in years.

She didn't want him to jerk her back to reality with guilt-ridden explanations about why he didn't go to Bill's funeral, or come back for William's christening.

She *knew* how guilty and responsible he felt. She knew because he was that kind of guy. He took the heat, the hits, the blame. Not in some arrogant, look-how-responsible-I-am way, either. When he succeeded, he did so quietly, without fanfare.

When he failed, he handled that quietly, as well.

By the time all that had flitted through Aimee's head, Matt's initial shock had faded.

He leaned forward and kissed her back. As fully and enthusiastically as she'd kissed him. He didn't waste any time hesitating or testing her reaction.

He *kissed* her.

And she discovered that beneath Matt's ordinary-guy veneer ran an undercurrent of passion, need and sexual hunger far greater than she'd imagined. His heart beat strongly, rapidly, vibrating through her as his mouth moved over hers with authority and exquisite gentleness. A thrill of unexpected desire pulsed through her all the way to her core. She leaned closer, yielding to the promise of his kiss.

But then he stopped. He lifted his head and hovered there, his lips so close to hers that their warmth still lingered on her mouth.

"Matt?"

He was frowning, his eyes as black as coals. "What are we doing?" he whispered.

Chapter Nine

A twinge of uncertainty embedded itself beneath Aimee's breastbone at Matt's question.

Don't ask what we're doing, she wanted to say. *Don't make it more than it is—or less.*

But she didn't have the courage to say that, so she tried to make light of it.

"Staying warm?" Her eyes had adjusted to the darkness, so that she saw the uncertainty there.

He smiled, but the worry didn't leave his eyes. His gaze roamed over her face, as if he were searching for something. "I'd really like to talk to you about—"

Aimee put her fingers over his mouth. "Please don't. Not now. I need to concentrate on William."

"Sure. Of course." He pulled away. "Sorry."

"Don't do that. Don't get all honorable and responsible on me."

"I'm confused," he said. "I'm not sure what you want from me."

She took a deep breath. "I'm tired and cold and

scared, and I'm feeling very alone." She nibbled on her lower lip for a second. "Is it possible I want the same thing from you that you want from me?"

Matt's eyes widened, and then narrowed. He sat unmoving for a moment, and then touched her chin with his forefinger. "I never meant to come on to you. I didn't intend to let this happen."

"I know that. Me, either. But it's happening." She looked down. "At least it is for me."

"Aimee—"

She looked at him from under her lashes, hearing his unspoken plea. "Just hold me for a little while. Hold me and keep me warm."

"No problem," he said with a sigh. "No problem at all." He settled back against the rock and cradled her against his side. His other hand held her head against his chest, and she felt him press a kiss against her hair.

She could hear his heartbeat, steady and fast. After a few moments, Aimee felt his thumb sliding across her cheek in a rhythmic, sweet caress. She sighed and curled her fingers against his chest. When she did, his heart sped up and his breaths turned ragged.

He stiffened, and she knew he was aroused. If she stirred, or if he did, she'd find out for sure just how turned on he was.

IT SURPRISED HER just how much she wanted to find out.

She knew Matt almost as well as she'd known her own husband. Probably better than any other man she'd ever met. He wanted her. His body told her that. But he would never act on those feelings.

He valued honor and loyalty above all else. In his

mind, acting on sexual feelings for his best friend's widow was a betrayal of her trust in him.

If she left it up to him, the stolen kiss and this warm embrace were as far as he would go. But even if she regretted it later, right now she wasn't willing to stop.

Heaven help her, she wanted more. Much more. The thought of touching him sent a thrill of desire humming through her. Her breath caught and her pulse raced.

She turned her head and pressed a soft kiss to the sensitive underside of his chin, feeling a triumphant satisfaction when he gasped quietly. Then she shifted, to gain easier access to his mouth.

For an instant, he sat still and unyielding, but she persisted, kissing his mouth and cheek, wrapping her arms around his neck.

Finally, he dragged her across his lap and gave her back kiss for kiss, caress for caress, until both of them were out of breath.

Matt lifted her again, and somehow she ended up lying on her back with him hovering over her. After a searching look, he lowered his head and kissed her again.

She'd never experienced anything like the feeling of his mouth on hers, of his body pressed against hers. He was aggressive and gentle at the same time. Demanding and giving. He rested his weight on his elbows so he could look at her. His erection pulsed against her thigh.

She slid her hand down his ridged abdomen until her palm found his hardness. The feel of his erection, firm and vibrant against her fingers, even through the barrier of his clothes, sent desire thrumming through her like a drumbeat.

He shuddered, and she knew he was almost to the edge. He felt for the buttons on her pants while at the same time his tongue slid over the sensitive skin of her neck. When his teeth scraped her earlobe and his breath warmed her ear, her whole body contracted in erotic reaction.

By the time she realized her pants were gone, his fingers were sliding inside the waistband of her underwear. Before he even touched her, she was gasping for breath.

Then his fingers reached their goal. She cried out.

He stopped, but she moaned in protest. "Matt, please. I need to feel you, too."

His dark eyes searched her face. Then he sat up, disposed of his pants, and stretched his length against her again.

Her backside was cold, pressed against the poor insulation of a thin blanket, but Matt's legs, his torso, his groin, radiated heat. His erection, hard against her, burned her skin with a delicious heat that turned her insides to liquid fire.

She closed her fingers around him, feeling his velvety hardness jump in her hand. At the same time his fingers slid through her nether hair and raked gently along the folds that hid her center.

She arched, the pleasure almost painful in its intensity. Pleasure she hadn't felt for far too long.

He teased her there, circling and coaxing, dipping and withdrawing, again and again, as his mouth traveled from her neck to her collarbone and on, to find the tip of her breast and nip at it through the thin silk of her long-sleeved pullover.

Then he lifted himself and settled between her

thighs. His rigid shaft rubbed against her, driving her desire. She opened to him, oblivious of the chilled air and the icy cold ground.

Bending his head, he nibbled at her lips, then pulled back and looked into her eyes.

"You okay?" he whispered.

In answer, she arched her neck and reached for his mouth with hers. "I'm ready," she whispered against his lips, knowing what he would know within seconds. Her core was liquifying, flowing, preparing to receive him.

He looked deeply into her eyes as if searching for something, then with deliberate, torturous slowness, he sank into her.

She moaned as his full length filled her and spread exquisite longing like golden, fluid light through her body. Enveloped in a haze of erotic sensation, all she could do was feel.

He stayed there, buried in her, his face tucked into the hollow between her neck and shoulder, for an interminable time. The feel of his breath on her neck was, if possible, more intimate than the sensation of his hardness filling her. It was a gesture of surrender, of trust, she realized.

He was blind with his eyes tucked into the darkness. He was vulnerable with his neck exposed to possible enemies. He was open, undefended.

Her eyes filled with tears. She slid her hand around the nape of his neck, and turned her face toward his.

Then he moved, and her body spasmed, sending electric shocks of pleasure tumbling through her. He slid out, out, until he hovered at her opening, then in to fill her again. The slow friction increased her wetness and made each successive thrust easier.

Each time he pushed into her, he sped up slightly, his body coaxing hers to keep pace with him. He stayed suspended above her, watching her. She realized that he was gauging her response and tailoring his movements to hers.

When she thought she would burst with anticipation, when her breasts were puckered and tight and her entire body felt electrified, he sat back on his haunches and pulled her legs atop his thighs. Then he held on to her waist and thrust again and again, filling her more completely and more deeply than she'd ever imagined possible.

Faster, deeper.

At last, he wrapped his arms around her and lifted her upright. He held here there, suspended, until she whimpered with need, then lowered her onto him. His powerful thighs flexed as he thrust upward.

Aimee gasped and cried out as a place inside her that had never been touched shattered. Matt kissed her, swallowing her breathless cries. Then he came, too, violently and thoroughly, his jaw clenched and his eyes squeezed shut as he poured everything into her.

With one last powerful thrust, he rocked with her and against her, continuing the dance as their climax faded.

After a few seconds of sitting there, draped against each other in the afterglow of sexual fulfillment, he splayed his fingers over her back again and gently lowered her to the ground, following her and settling beside her.

She lay her head on his shoulder as tears filled her eyes and ran over the bridge of her nose.

He touched one with his thumb and smeared it across

her cheek. "What's happening here?" he said tenderly. "Is something wrong?"

She shook her head slightly. "No. Nothing."

He kissed her forehead while his thumb swirled over her skin, spreading and drying the dampness.

"Then why are you crying?"

She shrugged and bit her lip to keep from saying *because this is a special occasion.*

MATT WOKE UP cold and stiff. Something sharp was poking him in the back. Something soft and sweet-smelling was pressed against his chest and side. He'd been dreaming about Aimee.

Aimee. He opened his eyes and discovered that his dream had come true. She was asleep with her head on his chest. Her brown hair was wavy and soft, and it tickled his nose. He'd kissed that hair, that brow, those lips.

Carefully, he lifted his arm and glanced at his watch. Almost seven. They'd slept for over two hours. The realization disturbed him. He'd left himself—and, more importantly, Aimee—vulnerable and exposed. The makeshift shelter was a pathetic cover. Had anyone happened by, they'd have been caught or killed.

He lay still for a moment and listened. He heard nothing but the wind whistling through the naked tree branches, and the muffled silence of falling snow. Occasionally, he heard a branch crack and fall, weighted down by snow and ice.

Aimee stirred and murmured something in her sleep. Matt ran his palm lightly down her silk-covered arm as his heart squeezed in regret.

He'd done worse than leave her vulnerable by falling

asleep on watch. He'd taken advantage of her by making love with her. She was completely dependent on him to keep her safe. She was frightened for her baby. And he'd promised to take care of her.

Instead, he'd let his feelings get involved. He'd acted on his personal desire, rather than in her and her baby's best interest. He'd relaxed his vigilance and put her in danger.

Despite his self-recrimination, his brain replayed the highlights of those few stolen moments—the supple firmness of her skin, her heavy breasts with their swollen nipples, the way she opened to him as he sank hilt-deep inside her.

To his dismay, his erection grew and strained, the physical symbol of his betrayal of her. He'd never allowed himself to be close to her, afraid that she or Bill or someone who knew them would see the truth in his face—how smitten he'd always been with her. He'd never even admitted to himself how much he'd wanted her.

Until now. He closed his eyes and clenched his jaw, forcing his brain back to his mission. Carefully, he slid his arm from around her and sat up.

She stirred, so he pulled the corner of the mummy bag over his lap to hide his erection, disgusted with himself.

She opened her eyes and looked at him in sleepy confusion. Then her eyes widened. He stared, mesmerized by the myriad emotions that flitted across her features.

To his surprise, she didn't turn away in disgust, or scream for help. Finally, she scraped her lower lip with her teeth and dropped her gaze.

Embarrassed? Humiliated? *Afraid?*

"Aimee, I'm sorry."

Her eyes snapped back up to lock with his. "Sorry?"

He nodded miserably. "We need to dress. It's almost dark, and I want to watch the cabin for a while before we make our move."

She shivered, and then ducked her head, searching around the cramped space for her clothes.

Matt turned the other way and dressed. Then he checked his MAC-10 to be sure it hadn't gotten wet, and loaded it. He did the same with the Glock and handed it to Aimee, handle first.

"Remember. From this point on, there's a chance you'll have to shoot someone to save your life or William's. You have to decide now whether you can do it. Don't aim if you're not prepared to shoot. And don't shoot if you're not prepared to kill."

She nodded, accepting the gun and sliding it into the paddle holster she'd already put on. As soon as she'd finished dressing, she started rolling up the blankets.

Matt stuffed them into his homemade pack and then took the mummy bag's stuff-sack from Aimee and packed it.

The sound of a motor starting up echoed across the canyon. He froze, listening. The motor revved once, twice. He touched Aimee's arm.

"Stay right here."

"Matt—"

"Stay here, and don't make a sound."

He carefully pushed the blanket aside and slipped out. When he'd sneaked as close to the edge of the overhang as he dared go, he used his eyes like an eagle or a hawk would to strafe the ground and search for prey.

Down below, Kinnard was on the snowmobile. As he watched, Kinnard revved it again, then turned off the engine. He cursed as he climbed off the vehicle and stomped back toward the cabin.

Had he forgotten something?

Without moving a muscle he didn't need to, Matt groped in his backpack until his hand closed around his binoculars. He pulled them out and watched Kinnard mount the snow-covered steps.

As the kidnapper reached for the door handle, a loud crack rang out, practically over Matt's head.

Kinnard whirled and looked in their direction. Matt didn't move. A huge branch crashed noisily as it fell through lower branches. It hit the ground not ten feet away from him with a deafening thud.

Kinnard stood perfectly still, watching and listening. His head was raised and his gaze was on the trees that were still swaying as they rebounded from being hit by the falling branch.

Matt knew that where he sat was partially obscured by tangled underbrush. He also knew that if he moved, Kinnard's brain would separate his gray-and-green-and-white camo from the surrounding natural foliage.

Behind him, he heard Aimee stirring.

It took every ounce of willpower he possessed not to move or speak.

Stay still, Aimee.

Matt didn't take his eyes off Kinnard as the man squinted up at the place where the branch had fallen. Behind him, Aimee continued to move. If she decided to push the blanket aside, they'd be sitting ducks.

Finally, the kidnapper's rigid stance relaxed. He

glanced around, then went inside the cabin. Matt didn't dare move. If Kinnard was just retrieving something he'd forgotten, he'd be out within seconds. Sure enough, Kinnard appeared again almost immediately, climbed on the snowmobile, started it up and headed northeast. Matt got a glimpse of the rifle in its scabbard, attached to the right side of the vehicle.

His breath hissed out between his teeth. He lifted the binoculars again and examined every inch of the cabin. As he was studying the layout and trying to remember anything he could about the couple of trips he and Bill had made up here when they were kids, a dim light came on in one of the windows.

His pulse sped up as a young woman appeared, holding a baby. She was rocking from one foot to another and bouncing the boy in her arms. As he watched, she bent her head and kissed him on his forehead.

A frisson of relief slithered down his spine. The woman's stance and demeanor were that of a caregiver. A nanny, maybe. Or a mother. She was obviously caring for William.

Aimee's baby was in safe hands—for the moment.

He sent up a brief *Thank You* prayer as he turned his gaze back to the northeast. The hum of the snowmobile's motor was waning. Kinnard was gone, at least for a while.

They needed to make their move now.

He detached the blanket from over the shelter opening and rolled it up. Aimee had searched the inside of the shelter to make sure they weren't leaving anything.

"Got everything?" he asked, looking around.

"I think so. What was that motor?"

"It was Kinnard on his snowmobile. He just took off

on it." Matt took her arm. "Aimee, as far as I can tell, right now William is in there alone with a young woman who appears to be taking *very* good care of him."

"Really?" Her gaze zeroed in on the cabin. "You saw him? He's all right? Can I see? Oh, Matt. Can we go now?"

"Listen to me. We've got to act fast. Kinnard headed north. He may be planning to hide up there and watch for us."

Matt rubbed his thumb across his lower lip and looked up at the sky. "The snow is coming down harder, so that's on our side. If we circle around to the south side of the cabin, and the snow keeps up, we should be able to sneak into the cabin without him seeing us."

"What about the girl?"

"When I saw her, she didn't act as if she were being watched. There didn't appear to be anyone else there, either. She was totally concentrated on the baby. But we have to go in as if there were armed guards in every room." He set his jaw and looked Aimee straight in the eye.

"That means you can't go rushing to William. You have to stay with me and do exactly as I say." He gripped her arms. "Can you do that?"

Her eyes glittered with dampness. She opened her mouth but nothing came out.

"Can you?" he growled. "Because if you can't, you're going to have to stay up here, hidden, until I can get him. I can't take care of both of you at once."

Chapter Ten

Aimee closed her eyes and took a deep breath. Then she lifted her chin. "I can do it."

He pushed away his need to touch her, to pull her close and kiss her and promise her that everything was going to be all right. This was a mission—he needed to act like a commander. And somewhere inside him he had to find the detachment and focus that made him good at his job.

And Aimee had to act like a soldier.

"This is a covert operation, Aimee. I'm the commander and you're my team. You follow my orders. If I say *abort*—then we abort the mission and retreat. Is that understood?"

Her lower lip trembled visibly, and her eyes glittered with unshed tears. But she nodded.

"Are you sure? Because if I give the order, you have to leave William and do what I tell you. Can you do that?"

Her chin lifted. "Yes, sir."

Fierce longing and aching compassion took his breath

away. For one instant, he abandoned his Special Forces training and allowed himself to be just a man. He cupped her cheek and leaned in to kiss her trembling lips.

When their lips touched, a thrill swirled through him that nearly buckled his knees. "I swear to God, Aimee, if you can trust me, I will save your baby."

She pulled away and gave him a solemn look. "I trust you," she whispered.

IT TOOK THEM forty minutes to trudge down the hill and around to the south side of the cabin. Despite what Matt had told Aimee, he was hampered by her. If he'd thought for a minute he could have safely left her in the shelter while he rescued William, he'd have done it.

If he'd thought he could wait until he could get a message through to Deke to fly a man in to help him, he'd have done that. But he had no time, and more importantly, no intention of leaving Aimee to fend for herself for even a short while.

He had to rescue them both.

So he clenched his jaw and moved at a pace far slower than he wanted to. As they approached the south, downhill side of the cabin, he quickly repeated his instructions to Aimee.

"I'll go in first. You wait for my hand signal. I'll wave you on as soon as I can verify that the room is clear. If you don't see me, you stay right where you are until you do." He looked at her evenly.

"What do you do if I don't come back out?"

She swallowed. "After ten minutes, I head for the door and—and give myself up." She paused. "Matt—?"

"No. No questions. You give yourself up."

She nodded reluctantly.

"Okay, once we're inside—do you remember what I told you about the layout?" He was going by what he remembered from his early teens. He hoped to hell he was at least partly right.

"The big room is in front. The right-hand door goes to a bedroom, the left-hand door goes to the kitchen."

"Right, and the kitchen is where I saw the girl holding William."

"You're going through the bedroom and around to the kitchen from the north side. You'll wait until I go in through the south door and surprise her. When you hear me speak, you'll come through the north door."

"Good. After that, just listen to me. I'll tell you what to do."

She nodded.

He looked at her and sent her what he hoped was an encouraging smile. "Ready?"

Aimee's throat closed up, but she nodded. A week ago, if anyone had told her she'd be part of a mountain rescue mission to save her own son, she'd have called that person insane.

Now, here she was, ready to stage a dangerous rescue at the side of a Special Ops soldier who was one of the best search-and-rescue specialists in the country.

They were about to rescue her seven-month-old son from kidnappers.

A trembling started deep within her and quickly spread out to her hands, arms and knees. She held on to the Glock with both hands, hoping it would give her strength and courage.

In front of her, Matt stole forward, his entire body

tense with expectation. He was ready for anything. His broad shoulders looked strong enough to support the world. His body, even in the bulky coat and camo pants, moved with the powerful grace of a big cat—a leopard maybe, or a cougar.

He was so strong yet he could be so gentle. She knew if anyone in the world could save her baby, Matt could.

Dear heavens, she trusted him. And she believed him—believed every word he said. She hadn't wanted to. She certainly didn't want to believe that he couldn't have prevented Bill's death. It was so easy to blame someone.

He turned his head and glanced at her over his shoulder, his profile strong and assured as a warrior. Then he gestured, waving her forward and pointing to an evergreen.

She rose to an uncomfortable crouch and eased forward, staying in the shadow of the tree. Her pulse sped up and her mouth went dry. She reached behind her and seated the paddle holster, making sure it was secure.

Matt shifted his weight to the balls of his feet, then held up his hand, thumb and first finger forming an O for OK.

She sent him the same gesture back.

He pointed to his own head and then forward.

He'd given her the five-minute crash course in signals, so she knew he was telling her that he was about to move forward. He didn't look back at her, so her responding nod was wasted.

As he half crawled, half crept toward the two steps that led to the cabin's door, she waited. Her limbs twitched with the need to move, and her pulse sped up.

She fought to keep her breathing even as she watched him unlock the door and slip inside. He'd warned her that once he'd disappeared into the house, she'd feel an almost uncontrollable urge to follow him.

It's the hardest thing to learn about stealth reconnaissance, he'd explained. *When your commander gives you an order, his life and yours rest on him being able to trust you to carry out that order, even if all it means is that you stay still.*

She'd thought she understood. But he was right. She burned to move a few steps forward, enough to be able to see through a window.

She set her teeth and clenched her fists. She would not move. As much as it was killing her not to be able to see what he saw, not to be able to lay eyes on her baby. Her scalp burned, and despite the cold air, a drop of sweat ran down her back.

"Come on," she muttered. "Hurry up."

MATT STOOD in the front room of the cabin, listening. He heard water running, and a feminine voice talking in low, soothing tones. Then he heard a giggle and a splash.

The girl was giving William a bath. The excruciating tension in his shoulders and neck relaxed, sending a rush of relief through him all the way from his head to his feet.

William was safe and happy.

He needed to take a look at the kitchen before he gestured Aimee in. He didn't want to leave her outside any longer than he had to, but he'd ordered her to treat this like a mission, and he had to do the same thing.

It was dangerous to leave her out there undefended, but that's how he would handle it if she were a BHSAR specialist. Except that if she were a specialist, she'd know how long to wait and when to move, even if she didn't get a signal.

Matt glided forward a few steps and peered in past the door hinges. Although the light given off by the oil lantern was dim and flickering, his narrow view caught the edge of the sink. He saw William's arms waving, and the girl's hand gliding a soapy washcloth over his pink, new skin. She laughed. She sounded young, maybe not far out of her teens.

Hopefully that was a good sign. If she were young and enchanted by William, chances were she'd be easily manipulated into talking about Kinnard.

He angled his head enough to get a view of the rear door to the kitchen. In the dimness it was impossible to tell if it was unlocked, but at least he'd remembered the cabin's layout correctly. There *were* two doors to the kitchen.

He retraced his steps across the room, thankful that the floorboards were solid, not creaky. He slipped through the front door and closed it. Then he gestured for Aimee.

She rose and moved stealthily forward and up the steps. He let out the breath he'd been holding. Thank God she was all right. He'd only taken a few seconds to reconnoiter, but he knew all too well that it took only a few seconds to kill.

"They're in the kitchen," he whispered in her ear. "She's bathing William and he's happy. He's splashing water everywhere."

She swallowed and then nodded. "Bath time is his

favorite time of day. He thinks it's funny to splash water on me—" Her voice cracked.

"It's okay, Aimee. He's right there and he's safe. Now—I'm going around through the bedroom. Give me sixty seconds and then step through the left door— that's the door to the kitchen—get the drop on the girl. And be careful."

She hadn't taken her eyes off the door. He understood why. Her baby was on the other side of it. "Don't take your eyes off her for an instant and—" he touched her chin, forcing her to look at him "—don't let yourself get distracted by William. It's important, Aimee. Your life and his depend on it. Our mission is to rescue him. Right now you've got to be a soldier, not a mother. Do you understand?"

Pain lit her eyes, but she nodded.

"By the time you get the drop on her, I'll be coming in the rear door and we'll have her in a cross fire. Okay?"

"How will I know sixty seconds?"

He counted for her. "Count like that. Don't let your anxiety let you speed up the count."

She nodded. "Okay."

"One final thing. Get her to sit down. Keep away from the window. I saw her. That means Kinnard might be able to see you. Let's go." He peered around the door and then pushed it open. He gestured for her to go to the left door and he'd go to the right.

He pointed at his watch, indicating that she should start counting.

She nodded.

He slipped through the door and took a couple of

precious seconds to study the bedroom. He'd give just about anything to find something that identified Kinnard's first name or any information about him or the girl. But the most remarkable thing about the room was the pile of pillows on the bed.

He crossed to the bathroom, which led from the bedroom onto the enclosed back porch.

Good. He'd remembered the layout.

The porch had a half-paned door and two windows. Directly in front of the back door was the door to the kitchen. Through it he could hear the girl talking to William, but he couldn't make out what she said.

Come on, Aimee. He looked at his watch and saw that she had twenty more seconds. He itched to get in, grab the baby and handcuff the girl before she knew what hit her. But he needed Aimee there to take her baby.

So he waited and watched the second hand crawl around.

FIFTY-NINE, SIXTY. Aimee took a deep breath, trying to control her anxiety. She adjusted her two-handed grip on the Glock, laid her shoulder against the door and took a deep breath.

"Here we go, pretty boy," the girl said. William gurgled happily.

Aimee's throat spasmed and her heart squeezed so tightly it hurt. *Her baby.* She almost cried out loud. Closing her eyes, she drew in another deep breath, and shouldered the door open, leading with her weapon.

"Don't move!" she snapped.

The girl shrieked and clasped William to her chest. "What? Who—?" She stepped backward.

"I said—don't move." Aimee's nervousness was completely overshadowed by the horror of what she was doing. She swallowed against the bile that rose in the back of her throat. She'd never aimed a weapon at anyone in her life. Yet here she was, threatening a pretty young woman who was holding *her* baby.

She was aiming a loaded gun at William—her own son. The thought and the action made her physically ill. She looked at the door behind them, absently noticing a pair of snowshoes hanging on a hook.

Where was Matt?

The woman shifted William to her other arm. "Who are you? Where—where did you come from?"

"I'm asking the questions," Aimee snapped. "What's your name?"

In the flickering lantern light, Aimee could see that the young woman's hair was a flat beige color, and her shocked dark eyes were rimmed with pale lashes, which made her look younger than she probably was. She opened her mouth but nothing came out.

"I asked you what your name is."

"Shellie," she said, her voice rising in pitch. She hugged William tighter. "It's Sh-Shellie. What's going on? Who are you?"

Aimee gestured with the barrel of the pistol. "Sit down."

Shellie started around the table.

"No. Sit here." Aimee glanced at the window over the sink, where tie-back curtains hung. She needed them closed.

"Hold it," she snapped.

Shellie froze.

"First, close the curtains." She gestured with the gun.

Watching her warily, Shellie tucked William into the crook of one arm and reached for the curtain ties with the other.

As soon as the fabric fell into place, obscuring the window, Aimee gestured again.

"Now sit."

Shellie obeyed. She bounced William on her lap.

Aimee's sore heart filled to bursting with equal amounts of joy and pain. Joy because her baby was obviously safe and happy. But her arms ached to wrap around his soft, plump little body.

She shivered. The kitchen was much warmer than outside, but she could feel a chilly breeze. "Why aren't you using that generator?"

Shellie looked from the baby to her and back again. "I had it on earlier. We're low on fuel."

Aimee glanced at the door to the porch. What was Matt doing? More than anything, Aimee wanted to lay her weapon down and take William away from Shellie, but she'd promised Matt she'd act like a soldier.

He'd given her an order, and he expected her to carry it out. She had to hold Shellie at gunpoint until he came in.

She quickly glanced around the kitchen, squinting in the dimness. Near the cabinets on the other side of the stove was a step stool. She lowered her head and crept across in front of the window, then nudged the stool closer to the kitchen table and sat on it. Her hands were getting tired, so she set the gun on her lap and rested one hand on the grip. The barrel was still aimed at Shellie.

Matt hadn't told her to talk to the girl, but he hadn't told her not to, either. "Who hired you?" she demanded, her gaze still hungrily assessing every inch of her son's body, to make sure he was all right.

Every time she spoke, his blue eyes turned her way. It was the hardest thing she'd ever done not to look at him. If he started crying, she didn't know if she could stop herself from picking him up.

"Hired me? I don't—"

"Don't lie to me." She picked up the Glock and aimed it at the girl's head. "Who brought you up here and left you to take care of—" Aimee paused. "What's the baby's name?"

She didn't want Shellie to know the baby was hers. If the woman knew that, it would give her a weapon that Aimee couldn't counter.

Shellie licked her lips nervously and lifted William to her shoulder. She patted his back. "I don't know his name. My boyfriend brought me up here. Listen, please don't hurt the baby."

Aimee uttered a short, ironic laugh. "Don't hurt the baby? Oh, don't worry, Shellie, I'm not going to hurt the baby. But if you don't give me some straight answers, I am definitely going to hurt you."

"Okay, okay." Shellie licked her lips again. "My— my boyfriend told me he needed me to watch his—his niece's little boy for a few days. She's sick, and—"

"I said, the truth!"

"But that *is*—"

"You really believe you're up here on the top of a mountain in a snowstorm because your *boyfriend's niece* has a cold?"

William's big bright eyes widened. He turned his head to look at her and frowned and began to whine.

Shellie's eyes grew wide and filled with tears. She sniffed. "You don't understand. When Roy tells you to do something, you don't get in his face about it, you know? I mean, he's been real good to me, but when he says do something, you just gotta do it." She shrugged and took her hand off William's back to wipe her nose on the sleeve of her sweater.

"Who's Roy?"

"He's my boyfriend. I told you."

"Roy who?"

Shellie's eyes narrowed, as if she were weighing the advisability of telling a stranger Roy's full name. Then her gaze dropped to the Glock and she swallowed. "Roy Kinnard. Look, did he do something wrong? 'Cause I didn't know nothing about it if he did. I just watch the baby."

Aimee lowered the gun again. It sounded like Shellie was completely in the dark about Roy's activities. But slim as it was, there was a chance that she was acting. Aimee's instincts told her to believe Shellie was telling the truth. But she couldn't trust her instincts. Not with her baby's life literally in the woman's hands.

"Oh, he's asleep," Shellie said softly.

Fierce longing arrowed through Aimee. She tamped it down. "Where does he sleep?" She kept her voice as hard as she could make it.

"In—in the bedroom. I pile pillows around him so he won't fall off the bed."

"You have children?"

Shellie laughed. "No, but I practically raised my two little brothers. I know all about babies."

Aimee wanted to call out to Matt, but she knew there must be a reason he was keeping quiet. What if something had happened? He'd told her to give herself up if he didn't show.

Apprehension stole her breath. She couldn't do that. She was here, in a warm, safe house with no one but a skinny girl standing between her and her baby. Right now she was in charge. She had the advantage, and she had to keep it.

"Put him to bed." Aimee aimed the gun at Shellie again.

Shellie stood carefully, still patting William on the back. She started toward Aimee, toward the closed door where Matt was supposed to be.

"No!" Aimee snapped. "The other way." She stood and blocked the door.

Shellie looked surprised, but she turned and stepped through the doorway into the big front room and across to the bedroom door.

Aimee was right behind her.

Shellie shifted William and reached for an oil lamp.

"No light." Aimee took a deep breath. "You do what I tell you to—nothing more," she ordered the girl. "I don't want any lights turned on. Just put Wi—the baby—to bed."

Shellie obeyed.

It broke Aimee's heart to watch another woman do the things she always did for William. Her heart twisted in agony to have him so close, and yet too far, in every sense of the word, for her to touch.

"There you go, darlin'," Shellie cooed. "Sleep

tight." She leaned over and kissed William's round pink cheek.

Aimee nearly lost it. She bit her lip—hard—to stop herself from moaning aloud. "Sit down, on the foot of the bed, and keep your hands in your lap, so I can see them."

She didn't want Matt to come into the kitchen and find nobody there, but she wasn't sure how concealing the kitchen windows were. Besides, she didn't think she could leave William alone, not even for a moment, now that she'd found him.

Aimee sat at the head of the bed, near William. She leaned back against the headboard and rested her gun hand on her lap.

"Now, how about telling me who Roy is and who he works for."

MATT PRESSED HIS BACK against the wall next to the half-paned door, his MAC-10 in his hand. He'd been about to burst in on Aimee and the girl when the clouds had parted, allowing the moon to light the snow-covered landscape.

Aware that Kinnard was still out there, probably waiting for a chance to ambush him, he'd flattened himself against the wall, and carefully surveyed the clearing around the cabin.

He wasn't worried about Aimee. As he'd listened to her barking orders and questioning William's caregiver, he'd smiled and his chest had swelled with pride. She was handling the girl like a pro.

He was relieved when Aimee directed the girl to take the baby into the bedroom. He would have much more freedom to handle Kinnard knowing that Aimee and William were out of the way.

Just as he'd decided it was safe to move across the porch to the kitchen door, he detected movement out of the corner of his eye.

He angled slightly, just enough to check the area close to the house. Nothing. Maybe he'd seen a rabbit or a deer, or even a wolf, but he didn't think so. His instincts, honed by four years in Air Force Special Forces, told him it was a human predator.

Crouching down, he crept across the porch to the door. He was taking a chance. If Kinnard saw the lantern's light, he'd know someone had opened the door.

But Matt would rather lure Kinnard to the kitchen than take a chance on him circling around to the front door. He wasn't about to get himself in a position where Aimee and William were between Kinnard and him.

Matt slipped into the kitchen. The lantern was still lit, although it looked low on oil. The curtains were closed but he knew his silhouette would be visible if he stood. So he slinked across the wooden floor to the table and extinguished the lamp.

He pulled his infrared glasses down from his forehead. He figured Kinnard was likely to have infrared glasses, too, so he stayed hidden as much as possible while he slipped back over to the porch door and opened it. Staying in the shadow of the open door, he rose enough to look out. The moon was still bright.

Then he spotted a figure sneaking down toward the house from the north. Matt recognized Kinnard's burly silhouette. His weapon was slung over his shoulder as he carefully picked his way across the snow from tree to tree.

Matt waited, watching. Once Kinnard got to the clearing, he'd have to step into the open to come any closer. Matt's fingers tightened on the MAC-10. He could take Kinnard out at any time. He'd used deadly force a few times as an Air Force Special Op, but always as a last resort. A *dead* last resort.

No, he wanted Kinnard alive. He wanted to find out who had hired him, and why. He knew he was capable of extracting every bit of information Kinnard had, if he were willing to apply the necessary impetus.

Still, to be safe, he kept a bead on the man as he paused at the edge of the trees. As Matt watched, the kidnapper pulled on a pair of infrared glasses, swung his rifle off his shoulder and held it ready as he stepped into the clearing.

As if on cue, clouds covered the moon. Without the glasses, Matt would be blind in the cloudy darkness. Yet he could see Kinnard's heat silhouette, and he tracked him across the snow-covered ground through his gun's scope.

Kinnard swung the rifle slowly across the windows and doors of the cabin. Matt ducked back into the shadow of the doorway as Kinnard swiveled the barrel his way.

He waited, counting the seconds, considering what he would do if he were the other man. After enough time had passed that the man should have moved on to survey the next window, Matt took a chance and peered out.

Sure enough, Kinnard was aiming at the far west window as he eased forward, his shadow crawling across the moonlit snow.

Matt took a deep breath and rapidly crossed the door's opening, flattening his back against the left facing. Now he was in a better position to shoot, if he had to.

He angled around the facing to get a better look at Kinnard's position.

A shot rang out—cracking the cold, silent air.

Kinnard went down.

Chapter Eleven

Aimee shot straight up off the bed at the sound of the gunshot. Before her brain could process the meaning of what she'd heard, several other shots followed—each one quieter than the last. *Echoes,* she realized.

But echoes of what? Matt's gun? Or Kinnard's rifle? Matt's gun was fully automatic, but she'd only heard the one shot and some echoes. That scared her—a lot.

Had Matt been shot?

William started to whimper. Shellie jumped up, reaching for him.

"Stop!" Aimee barked, pointing the barrel of the Glock at Shellie's head.

Shellie froze, her hands out, fingers spread.

"Don't move a muscle," Aimee whispered.

"That was a gunshot. It scared him," Shellie protested.

"Hush!" Aimee dared a quick glance at her baby. He hiccoughed and stirred, probably as much disturbed by the tension in the room as by the gunfire, then settled back to sleep. She held her breath and listened.

She didn't hear another shot, but a low deep rumbling rose from somewhere.

Shellie raised her head.

"What's that?" Aimee asked.

When Shellie didn't answer, she took a step toward her. "I asked you a question."

"It sounds like snow moving." Shellie licked her lips. Her fingers twitched, and her eyes darted back and forth from the gun in Aimee's hand to the baby.

Aimee moved away from her, toward the door that led into the living room. She didn't want to take a chance that Shellie would try to rush her and take her gun away. "You mean an avalanche?"

Shellie's dark eyes met hers. She nodded. "A small one. That gunshot may have dislodged the wet snow."

Panic fluttered in Aimee's throat. "Is it coming this way? What happens if it hits the cabin?"

Shellie shrugged. "This late in the year, when the weather's getting warmer, slides happen a lot. Can I pick up the baby? He's going to be scared."

Aimee looked at her son, then back at Shellie. *No, she wanted to say. He's my baby. I'll pick him up.* But the only thing she knew about this woman was that she cared for William. She wouldn't hurt him. What she would do to Aimee if she let down her guard, Aimee didn't know.

Doing her best to keep her face expressionless, Aimee nodded. "Have you got a safety seat?"

Shellie nodded. "Right there in the corner."

"Don't move. I'll get it." Aimee backed toward the corner and grabbed the child safety seat. She sat it on the foot of the bed near Shellie then backed away.

"Put him in it."

"Uh, ma'am? You're his mother, aren't you?"

Aimee froze. Was she that transparent? "Why would you say that?"

Shellie smiled as she strapped William safely into his seat. "I can see how he reacts to your voice. And you can't keep your eyes off him. I don't exactly know what Roy's doing, but I do know this baby needs his mama." She pushed the seat toward Aimee. "Take him. I know you're dying to."

Aimee forced herself to keep her eyes on Shellie. "No. I can't." She'd promised Matt that she could be a good soldier. William was safe. She didn't have to hold him to know that. Her hands tightened on the Glock's handle and she shook her head.

"He knows I'm here. And I know you've taken good care of him."

"I've been waiting for someone to get here. I called the police this morning, before Roy got here." Tears formed in Shellie's eyes and slipped down her face. "I know you don't trust me, but I did take care of him."

"You made the anonymous call?"

"Please don't tell Roy. He gets mad. But I was afraid something would happen to the baby."

"Thank you, Shellie," Aimee said, just as another deep rumble filled the air and she felt a shudder—she had no idea if it were the cabin floor or her own legs shaking, until she saw the lantern's flame waver.

Her fingers tightened on the Glock. First the gunshot and now an avalanche. Her head spun with panic and worry. Matt was out there. What if he'd been shot?

Had she found her baby only to lose Matt?

KINNARD HADN'T MOVED. Matt kept the MAC and his eye trained on the kidnapper's torso. Even with the infrared glasses, he couldn't tell if any of the shadows he saw were blood. And he couldn't risk going out to check.

Because the gunshot hadn't been from a Glock semiautomatic, or any other kind of handgun. That shot had come from a rifle at least as powerful as the one Kinnard carried. A gun he'd heard firing before.

It had to be Al Hamar, Novus's man who'd followed Matt back from Mahjidastan.

Kinnard had shot him back at the ransom drop point. Matt had seen the blood. But obviously Al Hamar's injury wasn't serious. It certainly hadn't kept him from following them.

Now he was trying to kill Kinnard. Matt had to assume it was because Kinnard was trying to kill Matt.

He'd be happy if Kinnard and Al Hamar got into a cross fire with each other, leaving Matt free to get Aimee and William to safety. But he knew it would be dangerous to let down his guard, so he crept back through the kitchen and into the front room. He wanted to check out the downhill side of the cabin and try to pinpoint Al Hamar's location.

Just as he started across the floor, he heard Aimee's voice, ordering the girl to precede her out of the bedroom.

As soon as he saw her, he spoke quietly. "Aimee."

Both women jumped.

"Matt! Are you okay?"

"Yeah. Shh. Get down, both of you."

"Where did that shot come from?"

"South. Below the cabin. I think Kinnard took a bullet."

"Roy?" the girl cried. "Roy's shot? Oh my God!" She set the baby seat down on the floor. One hand went to her mouth and the other pressed against her tummy.

"Calm down, Shellie," Aimee snapped at her. "Don't move."

Matt pushed his infrared glasses up onto his forehead and watched the two women's silhouettes.

"Is William okay?" he asked.

"He's fine. Shellie took very good care of him. Matt, she's the one who called in the tip."

"What? She called the police—?"

"Where is he? Where's Roy?" Shellie sobbed. "Is he in the kitchen?"

"He's outside," Matt said. "Settle down. We'll check on him as soon as I can be sure Al—the shooter—is gone."

"No! No!" Shellie ran for the front door.

"Shellie, wait!" Aimee cried.

"Hold it!" Matt said. "I need to ask you some questions about the kidnapping."

"No! I have to get to Roy! How could you shoot him?" Shellie broke for the door.

Matt dove for her but she got to the door first and slipped through, shoving it wide enough to block Matt and slow him down.

"Matt, stop her! She'll get killed." Aimee headed for the door.

"Aimee, no!" He stepped in front of her and caught her against his chest. "Get down! Get William."

Aimee immediately dropped to her knees and crawled back to the baby.

"Stay here. That's an order." Matt slid through the open

door and onto the front porch. Falling to his stomach, he held the MAC-10 ready to fire. He couldn't see anything.

He crept to the side of the porch, watching every direction. He didn't want to end up shot or captured. He still had work to do. He had to get Aimee and her baby off the mountain.

Shellie's voice sounded muffled and far away as she screamed for Roy. Matt needed to see around the side of the cabin, but the porch didn't extend to the corner.

He pulled down his infrared glasses again and scanned the area to the south. Nothing stood out that looked like a human. Sliding off the porch, he crawled westward along the cabin's wall, staying as much in the shadows as he could, keeping an eye out to the south for the shooter.

By the time he reached the southwest corner of the cabin, he could hear Shellie crying. Flattening himself against the cabin's wall, he peered around the corner and saw her crouched beside Kinnard, who was stirring.

He breathed a sigh of relief. Shellie was okay, and Kinnard was still alive. He needed to question them both.

While he watched, Kinnard sat up with Shellie's help. Matt saw a patch of black on the front of his winter camos. Blood. He must have taken a bullet in his shoulder, because he was moving pretty well. If he'd been hit in the chest, he wouldn't be upright.

Shellie rose to her knees, still holding on to Roy.

A tiny red dot appeared on the side of her head.

"Look out!" Matt yelled, breaking into a run. He risked a glance behind him, but didn't see anything.

He pushed his legs to pump as fast as possible through the wet snow. "Get down!"

He was about four feet away from the two of them

when Shellie turned her head in his direction. The red dot was centered on her forehead.

"Down!" Matt shouted. "Look out!"

Kinnard reached for her to try to pull her to the ground.

A loud crack drowned out all other sound. Shellie's head jerked, then slowly she toppled over.

"Shellie! Oh God!" Kinnard yelled, trying to get to his feet.

Matt saw the red dot slithering up Kinnard's chest and neck.

"Kinnard, duck!"

The kidnapper hit the ground and rolled sideways.

A second crack. Snow puffed as the bullet plowed into the ground barely two inches away from Kinnard's shoulder.

Matt dove into the snow and immediately raised up to shoot, but he knew his MAC wasn't powerful enough to reach the terrorist. So he hurled himself across the snow-covered ground and grabbed for Kinnard's rifle, but the sling was twisted around the other man's arm.

A third shot zinged past Matt's head. At the same time, Kinnard rolled again and sat up, trying to untangle the rifle sling. After a couple of seconds, he got it loose and raised the weapon to his uninjured shoulder.

"You SOB, your man shot Shellie!" Kinnard yelled.

"Not my man," Matt said. "You don't know him?"

"Hell, no. Who the bloody hell is he?" Kinnard bellowed.

"Tell me who hired you, and I'll get you to the cabin."

"Go to hell." Kinnard brandished the rifle in Matt's direction, but Matt grabbed the barrel and twisted it sideways, then shoved the end of it into the snow.

"Listen to me. Do you know who hired you?" Matt growled, aiming the MAC-10 at him. "Was it Margo Vick?"

Kinnard let go of the rife with a groan. "All I know is I was told where to go, when to get there, and how long I had to grab the kid before the alarm went off."

Another shot rang out and Matt and Kinnard both dove for the ground.

"You had to know who you were dealing with. You made the ransom call."

"I didn't do nothing but grab the kid and bring him and Shellie up here. The same guy who hired me told me to meet you for the ransom. He told me to kill the woman and the baby once I'd captured you. But Shellie wanted the baby—" He stopped. "Shellie!"

Just then a low rumbling that Matt hadn't noticed grew louder. He felt the ground beneath them tremble.

"Snowslide!" he shouted, scrambling to get his feet under him. He had to get to the cabin.

Kinnard cursed and began crawling toward the trees.

The rumbling grew in volume. Matt looked to the north, toward the peak of the mountain, and saw the white cloud foaming upward toward the heavens, obscuring the moon's light.

He was at least forty feet from the cabin. But about eight feet uphill was a sturdy-looking evergreen. Its trunk looked just about right for him to be able to hook his arms around.

He lunged forward, scrambling to get a foothold in the wet snow. He managed to shove his way through the branches and wrap his arms around the trunk as the first billowing drifts of snow reached him.

He ducked his head and locked his hands around the barrel of the MAC-10, praying that the steel and his fingers would hold.

But he was pretty sure he was going to be buried anyway.

Dear God, he prayed. *Let Deke find Aimee and her baby. Keep her safe.*

AIMEE HEARD THE ROAR and felt the ground shake.

Avalanche.

Muffled thuds jarred the walls and windows, rattling the glass. It was snow slamming into the cabin's walls.

"William!" she cried, throwing herself across the remaining foot or so of hardwood floor and grabbing his seat in her arms.

A vague memory from childhood tickled the edge of her brain. A children's education piece on what to do in a snowslide. The most important thing, she recalled, was to keep a pocket of air in front of one's face, and of course, not to panic.

She and William were inside, and probably safe, even if the cabin was buried, but what about Matt?

Dear heavens, he was out there with no protection.

She heard his voice as clearly as if he were next to her. *Take care of William. I'll take care of myself.*

You'd better, she answered silently. Holding on to William's safety seat, she crawled across the floor to the central wall that divided the kitchen from the bedroom. It seemed like it would be the strongest place to wait out the slide.

Provided the snow was heavy enough to crush the cabin, they might survive.

She lay down against the wall and cradled William's seat against the curve of her body.

"Hi, William Matthew Vick," she whispered, touching his cheek for the first time since he'd been kidnapped. "Smile for me," she coaxed. He waved his arms and cooed.

She leaned forward to kiss his little face. "That's right. I've been waiting a long time to see you, too." Her eyes filled with tears. She blinked and one fell on William's forehead. She wiped it away.

"Hang in there with me," she said softly. "I've got someone I want you to meet. He's a brave man. He took care of your daddy and he took care of me."

As she spoke the words, she realized that she meant them. Matt would have done everything in his power to save Bill—even sacrificed himself if it meant Bill could have lived to see his son. That was the kind of man Matt was.

She smiled sadly and blinked away her tears. "A very brave man," she whispered as the rumbling of the cascading snow grew louder and the cabin's timbers creaked and groaned.

Behind her, glass shattered. She pulled William closer and covered his seat with her torso and arms.

As THE SNOW PILED UP around Matt, he pondered whether the latest theory of surviving a snowslide made sense. It was called the Brazil nut effect. The theory was that, when shaken, larger and less dense objects rose to the top of water, snow or, in the case of Brazil nuts, the contents of a can of mixed nuts.

The idea was to let the moving snow shake you to the top as more dense rocks and limbs were plowed under. Many experts felt it made more sense than the theory of trying to swim by flailing one's arms.

The snow was piling up over his head, and his arms and legs were trembling, they were so tired. The tree's trunk was bent almost double and its roots were coming loose from the ground.

Matt figured that if the Brazil nut theory were wrong, he had two chances—slim and none. But he opted for optimism.

With a deep breath, and gripping the MAC-10 as tightly as he could with his exhausted, frozen right hand, he let go of the tree and let the snow carry him down the mountain.

Take care of William, he whispered silently to Aimee. *Don't worry about me.* As the snow billowed around him and he covered his nose and mouth with his left arm, warm tears mixed with the freezing crystals on his cheeks.

SUNDAY 0700 HOURS

MATT WAS FREEZING. He was afraid to move, afraid of finding out that he couldn't. For a few minutes, he lay doubled in on himself like a fetus, figuring that eventually he'd get up the courage to move. And he'd count himself lucky if his fingers and toes didn't break off when he wiggled them.

The sun was up. That surprised him. The last thing he remembered was floating on snow in the darkness. Now the sun felt warm on his shoulder and back. But strangely, there was also warmth below him. Warmth and sticky wetness.

Don't let it be blood.

Not yet brave enough to move, he assessed his position. His head, covered by his parka's hood, was tucked between his shoulders, and its hem was pulled down as far as it would go over his butt. He didn't remember doing any of that.

All he remembered was letting go of the tree and floating downhill on a wave of snow.

And praying that Aimee and her baby were all right.

Aimee!

He straightened—or he tried to. He couldn't move, and it wasn't just because his muscles were ice-cold.

Something was on top of him, weighing him down.

Snow? He took a deep breath, preparing to push against the weight, and his nostrils filled with the un-mistakable spicy smell of evergreen needles.

When he tried to move, pain shrieked along his nerve endings.

Nausea engulfed him. Sternly, he forced his brain to rise above the pain and think rationally.

One part of his body hurt more than all the rest, but for the life of him he couldn't figure out which part it was. The pain seemed to be everywhere at once. And the nausea was making it worse. He stuck out his tongue and lapped at a few snowflakes that were caught on his lips.

Then, carefully, he flexed his ankles, relieved that his brain still had that much control over his limbs, and waited. They weren't causing the nauseating pain.

After a few agonizing seconds, his cold calf muscles responded and relaxed. Matt blew out a breath. One by one, he tested each muscle without actually moving. Each time, he cringed and braced himself for the shriek-ing pain. It was a slow, excruciating process.

Finally, he concluded that his feet and legs weren't the problem.

Then he realized he hadn't opened his eyes. When he did, he saw the crisscrossed shadows of evergreen branches. Inhaling carefully, he smelled wood, evergreen—and blood.

Oh, hell. The sticky stuff was blood. Trying not to move his head, he looked down at himself, and saw where the blood was coming from.

A small branch was embedded in the meaty part of his left forearm.

He gagged and his mouth filled with acrid saliva as his stomach heaved. Icy sweat beaded on his face and trickled down the side of his neck. What if that wasn't the only branch that had impaled his body?

What if he couldn't get to Aimee and William?

Lying still, Matt racked his brain for a way to free himself from the tree.

He had a small handsaw in his backpack. He groaned in frustration. The backpack had burned up in the Hummer. What did he have on him?

A knife. In a scabbard attached to his belt. Now if he could just get to it.

In between several bouts of nausea and a couple of periods of unconsciousness, he finally worked the knife out of its scabbard with his right hand without ripping the stick out of his arm.

Once he had the knife in his hand, it was only a matter of about a half hour of excruciatingly slow and careful sawing to cut the thin stick loose from the branch. And then another thirty or forty minutes to extricate himself from underneath the branch. Afterward, he barely remembered anything about it, except for the awareness that he was taking much too long and bleeding a lot.

All in all, it was a miracle that he lived through it. And a miracle that the thin branch hadn't broken a bone. He shuddered, hoping the miracles didn't run out too soon, because he was pretty sure he was going to need a few more of them.

And as hard as he tried to pretend that it wasn't a problem having his forearm skewered on a stick, he knew better.

So much for miracles. With only one arm, he wasn't sure even a miracle could help him save Aimee and William. But he had to try.

As he put his right glove back on, he heard something. It was a baby—crying.

William!

He was close. At least he was close to them. His eyes filled with tears. Now all he had to do was figure out exactly where he was in relation to Aimee and the baby.

Looking around, he noted that whatever he was sitting on, it was a few feet above the surrounding snow. He blinked, trying to get his bearings. Maybe if he stood…

He tried to tuck his left arm against his chest, but the stick was in the way.

With a sick desolation, he faced the truth. He couldn't do anything until he got rid of the piece of wood. The good news was that it was barely more than a twig—maybe a half inch in diameter and around four inches long. The bad news was that four inches was hardly enough to grip.

With his right hand, he picked up a twig lying nearby

and put it between his teeth, then tried to view his impaled arm detachedly, as if it were someone else's.

For a few minutes, he bathed his forearm in snow, numbing it with cold.

Then, biting on the twig, he carefully wrapped his right hand around the two inches of bloody wood protruding from the inside of his arm. He took deep breaths until he was drunk on oxygen. Then with a roar, he slowly and deliberately pulled the stick out of his arm.

And passed out.

Chapter Twelve

Matt's arm hurt like hell. He opened his eyes and looked at the matching holes on either side of his forearm, where the stick had been.

He frowned. *Stick?*

Eventually, he remembered that his arm had been impaled on a small sharp branch, and that he'd pulled it out himself. Maybe it was a good thing that he didn't recall the specifics.

The two holes on either side of his arm were oozing blood. Another miracle. The stick hadn't shredded an artery.

He licked his dry, chapped lips and tried to sit up. Reflected sunlight nearly blinded him.

He looked down. He was sitting on something metallic. He brushed snow away to reveal a slab of tin.

A tin roof. He was on top of the cabin!

His whole body trembled in relief. That's why he'd heard William crying. Aimee and her baby were directly below him. All he had to do was get to a door or window. Then he could get them out and get them to the next rendezvous point and they'd be safe.

Rendezvous point. Deke.

Matt shook his head as trepidation churned in his stomach. How was he going to get them to the rendez- vous point? He wasn't even sure he could stand up.

He'd arranged for Deke to put down near the peak at 0900 hours. But since the last storm and the ava- lanche, he had no idea what conditions were like there.

He needed to talk to Deke.

Awkwardly digging into the inside pocket of his parka with his right hand, he pulled out the satellite phone. At least the sky was clear this morning. He pressed the call button on the phone. The light came on. Thank God the battery wasn't frozen.

He read the time on the phone's display. After 0800 hours.

He punched in Deke's number.

"Matt!" Deke's voice was distorted by static. "Son of a gun! What the hell's going on?"

"Deke." His voice was hoarse and shaky. He cleared his throat. "Are we on for 0900?"

Static filled his ear. He turned his head, trying to get a better signal.

"—don't know if I can—put down—"

"Deke," Matt shouted. "0900. 0900. Be there."

"—firmative—"

Deke was worried that the new snow would make it impossible for him to set the helicopter down near the peak, but he would be there.

It was up to Matt to make sure Aimee and William got there. Between them, he and Deke would figure out how to get them into the helicopter.

Matt checked the battery life of his phone. Not good.

It was down to one bar. He pocketed it and awkwardly pushed himself to his feet, holding his throbbing left arm close against his chest. The first thing he saw was the barrel of the MAC-10, sticking out from under a dusting of snow and partially hidden by the tree.

He grabbed it, wondering if the cold had rendered it useless. Then he scanned the landscape, assessing the slide's wreckage.

The slide had deposited what looked like about two feet of powder over the snow that had already fallen.

About twenty feet away, something stuck up at an odd angle from the snow. Matt shaded his eyes and squinted. It was a body, clothed in winter camo.

Kinnard. Damn. Based on the angle and rigidity of his body, he had to be dead and either frozen or in rigor.

Turning toward the south, he searched for any sign of Al Hamar, with no luck. His best estimate of when Al Hamar's rifle shots had come from put the terrorist beyond the worst of the piled-up snow. If he'd stayed put, he was probably unhurt.

Matt couldn't afford to assume that Al Hamar was no longer a threat.

Matt had to proceed as though the terrorist had survived the storm. He surveyed the whole visible landscape, but didn't see any new footprints, any disturbance of the new snow. He saw no sign that suggested anyone had been there.

Kinnard was dead. But Matt had to assume that Al Hamar was still out there somewhere. That meant Aimee was still in danger. Because although Novus needed Matt alive so he could be questioned, he had no use for Aimee or her baby.

Matt looked back at Kinnard's frozen body. This time he spotted the assault rifle, half buried in the snow. He needed that rifle. So he used a few precious minutes to trudge through the snow. He confirmed that Kinnard was dead. Then he dug the rifle out of the snow with his good hand.

Turning back toward the cabin, he examined the tree that had fallen onto the cabin's roof, and onto him. Its roots were still partially embedded in the ground. And that meant that only part of the tree's weight was resting on the cabin.

At that instant, the tree creaked and settled, shaking the cabin. Its movement drew his attention to a branch that had penetrated the roof in the same way the stick had penetrated his arm.

Dear God, don't let Aimee or William be hurt.

Matt cautiously approached the downhill side of the cabin. As he got closer, he saw the damage the big tree had caused. The sides of the cabin had been crushed.

The slight bump he saw in the roofline told him the central portion of the structure had withstood the weight of the tree better than the sides. But the way the tree was creaking and moving, its roots might give way at any minute, and its full weight would flatten the cabin.

He had to get Aimee and her baby out of there.

Cradling his hand, he climbed over the snowdrifts and landed on the porch with a thud, jarring the hell out of his arm.

The pain was like a punch to his gut. For a few seconds he couldn't get his breath as dizzying nausea racked him.

Then he heard William crying again. He couldn't tell

exactly where the sound was coming from, and ice crystals had formed on the panes of the door. He rubbed them away, trying to see inside.

"Aimee!" he called. "Aimee! Are you okay?" He couldn't see anything through the glass panes. The inside of the cabin was pitch-black.

"Aimee! Answer me!"

SUNDAY 0900 HOURS

THE HEAVY TREE that lay on top of the cabin shifted as the snow melted around it, and the roof creaked and groaned. Aimee shook her head as she stared at the huge branch that had speared through the cabin's roof right in front of the wall where she'd huddled with William. It had missed them by several feet, but somehow that wasn't comforting.

She jumped and cringed as a thud reverberated through the cabin. Another tree falling? She wasn't sure. All she knew was that the loud bang was the latest in a long night full of very scary sounds. Many of them from the cabin itself. The center wall where she'd huddled with William had turned out to be a very good choice.

When the tree had hit the cabin, glass had popped out of the windows and studs and logs had cracked loudly. Nails screeching against wood, and logs crunching under the weight of the tree, had continued all through the night.

Every screech, every crunch, had Aimee cringing and hovering over William to protect him, terrified that the cabin's structure wouldn't hold for another second.

She clutched William closer and whispered to him. "I know, William, I know. You're so uncomfortable.

Your mommy isn't taking very good care of you." She took a shaky breath. "You're wet and hungry, and all I've got is this cold bottle of formula."

Earlier, she'd dared to leave William long enough to weave her way into the kitchen around the debris. She'd found a bottle turned upside down on the drain board, with its top beside it. Further searching had yielded two cans of baby formula.

William had taken a little formula, but he scrunched up his face, making sure his mommy knew he didn't like it. That, plus his reaction to her fear, made him fussy.

She'd held him through the rest of the night, singing lullabies and trying to pretend for his sake that she didn't believe they were the only survivors of the snow-slide. Trying to believe that Matt was out there some-where, trying to get to them.

"Aimee!"

She stopped murmuring to William and listened. She'd dozed a few times during the night, only to wake up thinking she heard Matt calling her. But it always turned out to be the wind howling or the timbers of the house rubbing together.

"Matt?" It was foolish, she knew, to answer the wind, but there was nobody to hear her except William.

"Aimee? Are you all right?"

That sounded real. She held her breath, listening. Hoping with every fiber of her being that it really was Matt. At the same time fearing she was hallucinating. She was desperately afraid that he hadn't survived.

Then she heard a pounding on the door. She looked up, squinting against the glare of sunlight on snow.

Pushing herself to her feet, still clutching William to her chest, she forced her stiff muscles to move.

She had to thread her way around the limb that had impaled the roof, and between fallen beams and broken glass, but she finally got to the door. She rubbed frost off the glass. "Oh, dear heavens, Matt! It's really you."

"Aimee."

Standing in front of the door with the sun and bright snow behind him, he looked like an angel. The parka's hood was pushed back. His ears were bright red, his cheeks were chapped, and his mouth was compressed into a thin line, but he was there. And he was beautiful.

He grabbed the doorknob and pushed. It didn't move.

"Matt, the cabin's crushed—"

"Get away from the door." He put his right shoulder against it and shoved.

Something cracked, and a broken board fell, barely missing his arm.

"Matt, stop! You're going to get hurt." Aimee had never seen him so desperate.

He kicked away the board and pulled his MAC-10. "Get as far back as you can. I'm going to break the window."

"Wait!" Aimee yelled.

He stopped, surprised.

"Matt, the door's stuck, and the cabin is collapsing. Slow down. We need to figure out what to do."

He pressed a gloved hand against the glass. "Listen to me. We don't have time. Deke is going to be at the peak in less than ten minutes. I've got to get you and William up there."

Her first reaction was excitement. "Deke's coming?" They were safe.

But Matt's face told a different story. He looked exhausted, desperate, defeated.

Shifting William's weight to her right arm, she laid her left hand against his right on the other side of the cold glass.

"What's wrong?" she asked softly.

He laid his forehead against the glass. The corners of his mouth were white and pinched. "My phone is almost dead. I won't be able to contact Deke again."

Aimee heard what he didn't say. This was their last chance. "Break the windows," she said, and backed away.

He met her gaze. She wasn't sure what he was looking for in her eyes, but she knew by looking at him that his goal was the same as hers.

Get William to safety.

He swung the handle of the MAC-10 at the panes of glass.

She wanted to cry at the weakness of his swing. He was exhausted. He'd spent the night out in the freezing cold. He'd fought to get to them. She was terribly afraid that he was using up the last dregs of his strength to save her baby.

And she was going to let him do it.

Several blows later, there was a fair-sized hole in the door. Not large enough for her to get through, but plenty of room for William's safety seat.

"Matt, stop! That's enough." Without waiting to hear his response, she ran back to the wall and secured William into his safety seat. Then she took one of the blankets she'd used for warmth, and wrapped it around the seat.

When she looked up, Matt was bracing himself to swing again. "Get back," he shouted.

His hoarse voice and his pinched face attested to his exhaustion. He was hovering at the end of his strength.

Would he make it to the peak? She had to believe he would.

"Matt. There's no time. Here."

"What are you doing?" Matt cried. "Another couple of minutes and I'll have enough room to get you out."

"No. There's no time."

He stared at her as if he didn't understand what she was saying. After a second, he nodded.

She kissed William and took a precious few seconds to whisper to him. "I swore once I got you back in my arms I'd never ever let you go. You're the most important thing in my life. You *are* my life. But I can't keep you safe here."

She touched his chin and he giggled, which brought tears to her eyes. "That's right. It's too cold here. So Matt's going to take you someplace where you'll be safe, and I'll see you soon, okay? You can trust him. I do."

She kissed him one last time, then covered the seat with the blanket, and handed it through the broken panes to Matt.

When he reached out his right hand to take the baby seat's handles, Aimee saw the blood that stained the left sleeve of his parka.

"Matt, you're bleeding."

He shook his head. "Not so much anymore."

"You can't make it to the peak like this. What happened?"

His grim mouth flattened. The only color in his face came from the bright spots on his cheeks. "I'll make it. Stay inside. Stay warm. I'll be back for you," he rasped.

She blinked away tears. She touched his hand. "I know you will."

Gripping William's seat, he turned away.

"Matt," Aimee called.

He looked over his shoulder at her.

"I trust you."

For an instant, his gaze held hers, then he nodded and turned. He carefully maneuvered the sloping hill of snow in front of the cabin, holding tightly to the baby seat with his right hand.

Aimee watched him as long as she could. Finally, she had to accept that no matter how hard she strained, she wouldn't get another glimpse.

The man she'd once thought she could never count on now held her baby's fate in his hands. And she'd told him the truth.

She trusted him to keep William safe.

She moved back to the center wall, wrapped herself in the remaining blanket, and sat down to wait for Matt to return.

She didn't allow herself to consider that he might not make it back.

Above her, the snow-laden boards creaked ominously.

MATT HEARD THE HELICOPTER long before he saw it. The rhythmic drone of the propellers was strangely soothing. He matched his pace to the engine's cadence.

At least he was warming up. Probably the combined efforts of climbing and maintaining his balance with only one arm. Setting the baby seat on a downed tree trunk, he lifted the blanket slightly to check on William. It was the third time he'd peeked.

But no matter how much he lectured himself that he needed to keep the blanket in place so William didn't get cold, he found it impossible to go more than a few minutes without checking on him.

William was fussy and unhappy, but he'd stopped crying. That worried Matt.

Like he knew anything about kids.

He figured the baby was wet or hungry or both. He hoped that was all that was wrong. But as fussy as William was, whenever Matt checked him, his blue eyes latched on to Matt's and widened.

"Do you have any idea who I am?" Matt whispered. "I'm your godfather. Not that I deserve to be. I haven't done a very good job of taking care of you so far, but I'm hoping I can fix that in just a couple of minutes."

William waved his arms and whined.

"I know. It's cold. But you're about to have an adventure that possibly no man your age has experienced."

His mouth twitched. "That's right," he said. "You *are* a man. A little man right now, but a man. A brave, good man, just like your daddy."

At that moment, Matt noticed that the sound of the helicopter had gotten louder. The propellers appeared from the other side of the mountain, rising up like the cavalry coming over the hill in a B Western movie.

Matt sat the baby seat down and waved with his right hand.

Deke, in his supercool sunglasses and his helmet and earpiece, waved back. He maneuvered the bird so that he was hovering almost directly over Matt's head. The downdraft created by the propellers whipped around, lofting the blanket that protected William.

Matt knelt and tucked the corners of the blanket securely around the baby.

When he glanced up, Deke was holding up his satellite phone. Matt reached for his, hoping the battery hadn't died.

To his relief, he saw that its light was on.

"I'm glad to see you're still upright. The weather service reported an avalanche, and I could see the results when I flew in." Deke's voice was cut by static.

"I rode it. Kinnard and his girl didn't make it."

"Damn. Aimee and the baby okay?"

Matt nodded. "Drop a basket," he yelled into the phone. "You're taking the baby."

A surprised expletive slipped from Deke's lips. Then he recovered. "You got it. Be right back." The helicopter rose and angled away from the mountain peak.

Matt knew what he was doing. He needed room to hover on autopilot while he secured a rescue basket to a rope.

While he waited, Matt made sure that William was snugly strapped into his safety seat. Then he tucked the blanket in tightly. "Okay, William Matthew Vick. You ready for your great adventure?"

To his utter shock, William giggled. Matt couldn't stop himself from smiling. He pulled off his glove and traced the baby's plump cheek with his forefinger.

"You're as beautiful as your mother," he whispered, surprised when his voice broke.

Above him Deke was back, maneuvering until he

hovered directly over them, blasting them with downdraft. Then he lowered the heavy metal basket. Matt grabbed the cold steel.

Even the slightest movement made his arm shriek with pain. But the only way he could hang on to the basket was to embrace the line with his left arm.

He picked up William's baby seat and lifted it over and in, then grabbed the bungee cord that was attached to one side and ran it through the handles of the baby seat and secured it to the other side. By the time he completed those maneuvers, he was dizzy and sick with pain.

He looked up, still holding on to the cage, and waved at Deke, who gave him a thumbs-up.

Matt watched, not breathing, as Deke activated the crank that raised the basket. When it was close enough, Deke leaned out and grabbed it, lifting it in through the open door. Once the basket was safely inside, Deke sent Matt another thumbs-up, then held up his satellite phone.

Matt retrieved his phone.

"—the hell's wrong with your arm?"

"Forget it," Matt growled. "Get the baby out of here."

"What about you and Aimee—?"

"You'll have to put down."

Deke nodded. "Six hours?"

Matt had racked his brain about where Deke could safely set the helicopter down. The original secondary rendezvous place was a clearing two miles southwest from the cabin. It was probably the best choice.

"Secondary rendezvous," he yelled into the phone.

Deke shook his head and shrugged. "Wha—?"

The static was growing. Matt knew his phone was

about to go dead. "Secon—dary ren—dez—vous," he enunciated slowly.

Deke ducked his head, listening. Then nodded. "—dary—"

Relief nearly buckled Matt's knees. Deke had heard him.

"Deke," he yelled. "Anything on the sabotage?"

Deke shook his head and spoke, but all Matt got was static. He looked at his phone's display in time to see the battery light go out. It was dead. That was it. This would be the last communication until they were rescued.

If they were rescued. He waved the phone and shook his head.

Deke frowned and then held up six fingers.

He wanted confirmation of the time. *Six hours.* Enough time for as much snow as possible to melt.

Matt nodded and gave Deke the thumbs-up.

Deke returned the gesture, grinning. Then he held up his forefinger, followed by five fingers, then his closed fist, and his closed fist again.

1500 hours. Three p.m.

Matt repeated the signs with his right hand.

Deke mimed a salute, turned the helicopter and flew off.

Matt watched until it disappeared over the edge of the peak. Then he fell to his knees, his stomach heaving and clenching, although he had nothing in it. Then he raked up a small handful of snow and let it dissolve on his tongue, hoping the chill would chase away the queasy dizziness.

The pain in his forearm had become a constant

agony, made worse by the numbness in his fingers. He unzipped his parka and tucked his hand inside, hoping to warm his fingers without having to move them. He felt warm blood trickling down his cold arm. He shivered.

Then he staggered to his feet. He had to get back to Aimee. She'd be happy to know that William was safe.

He'd be happy if he could get her safely to the rendezvous point before he collapsed from blood loss.

Chapter Thirteen

It had been almost twenty-four hours with no communication from Kinnard. He hoped to hell the jerk hadn't run off with the money. He trusted him, but only so far.

He tried Kinnard again. No response. It wasn't the storm this time. The skies were clear. He tried Kinnard's girlfriend, too, but no luck there.

Maybe Parker had killed them.

He drummed his fingers on the computer table. Parker could certainly have killed Kinnard. From what he'd seen in the years he'd worked for Black Hills Search and Rescue, it was pretty obvious that Parker would do anything for one of his oath brothers—or for Aimee Vick.

But killing the girl who'd been brought in to take care of the Vick baby—that was another matter. Parker wouldn't have the stomach for that.

He stood, kicking his desk chair backward. Looking out the window at the Black Hills, he doubled his hands into fists and forced himself to stay calm. Hopefully, Kinnard and the girl were dead. If they'd turned tail and run, all his careful plans could be in jeopardy.

He picked up his prepaid cell phone and looked at it. He did not want to make this report, but he had to.

AIMEE SQUINTED against the glare of the sun on the brilliant white snow outside the cabin door, and swung the stick of firewood at it one more time. To her relief, the pane of glass finally broke.

The stick of firewood she wielded in her gloved hands was heavy, but the cabin's door was solid wood and the frames that held the six panes of glass were solid. Even the glass seemed to be reinforced.

She'd been working ever since Matt had left. She didn't have a watch, but she knew it had been a long time—maybe too long.

No. She wouldn't—couldn't—worry about William. Matt would die to save him.

She swung again, letting the reverberation of the blow shake that thought from her mind.

"Matt—won't—die," she muttered as she swung again and again. He'd promised her he'd be back. She believed him.

"He—won't—die." She dropped the log from her aching hands and blew out a breath.

She eyed the hole where the glass panes had been. It was big enough for her to crawl through—probably. But if she climbed out now, she'd have nothing to do but sit in the snow and wait for Matt to show up.

The roof creaked again, and Aimee cringed. The fear that had dogged her ever since the sun had begun beating down on the snow sent her pulse skyrocketing. What if the roof collapsed?

Maybe it was a good idea to go ahead and climb out.

She could wait for Matt outside in the sunshine, away from the possibility of being crushed when the tree's last clinging roots let go and dumped its full weight on the cabin roof.

She grabbed the daypack, and then remembered the food and drinks she'd seen in the kitchen. Running into the kitchen, she chose a few things to put in the daypack. Too much and it would be too heavy to carry. Then she went through the kitchen drawers, checking to see if she saw anything that might come in handy. She found a couple of odd-shaped pieces of metal that she assumed were key rings, a small can opener with no handles. She had no idea if it was broken or if it was made that way, but she stuck it in the bag anyway.

One of the drawers seemed to be dedicated to first aid supplies. She grabbed antibiotic ointment, gauze, tape and a small bottle of alcohol. Then she saw a pair of scissors and stuck them in the pack, as well.

Lifting the pack, she grimaced at its weight. "I'll ask Matt," she told herself. "He can dump whatever he thinks we don't need."

Back in the front room she examined the hole in the door and brushed away all the glass shards and splinters of wood she could see. Folding the blanket several times, she lay it over the bottom of the jagged opening.

Outside, drifts of snow glistened with water where the sun hit them.

She went back to the kitchen and grabbed a chair to drag over to the door, but stopped when she heard something. She glanced up, cringing. Had the tree's roots finally let go?

"Aimee?"

A thrill lanced through her. "Matt?" She whirled. There he was, on the other side of the broken door. Spots of color stained his cheeks, standing out against his pale skin and pinched mouth. His left hand was tucked inside his unzipped parka, and blood stained the sleeve—more than before.

"Matt!" She was stunned at his appearance. His face was set, with lines of pain etching it. His eyes were too bright, and appeared sunken. And his face was horribly pale. She pasted a smile on her face, trying not to show how worried she was about him. "Is William—?"

He nodded and a tight smile lightened his drawn features. "He's safe. Deke's got him." His voice was hoarse, and he was obviously trying to sound upbeat.

"You put him in the helicopter?"

"Actually, he rode up in a basket."

"A basket?" she repeated, horrified at the picture his words evoked.

"These are specially designed for rescuing people. Like the ones they used down in New Orleans during Katrina."

"Oh." She wasn't convinced about the safety, but if William was fine, then that's all that mattered.

He coughed. "I see you found something to do. You finished breaking in the windows."

"I figured it was about time for me to chip in."

"Let's get you out of there."

"You just stay back. I can do this myself."

He lowered his gaze and complied. That sent an

arrow of hurt through her. Not because she needed his help, but because he knew he was too weak to offer it.

She grabbed the daypack and lifted it through the broken window. Lowering it by one strap, she let it fall to the ground. Then she pulled the chair over.

Standing on it, she climbed through the broken panes and hopped to the ground. Then she picked up the blanket, shook it out and rolled it up.

"Leave it," he said.

"Are you sure? Because I can carry it—"

"Leave it."

She tossed the blanket back inside. "How far are we going?"

"About two miles."

"Two miles? That's not bad. Deke's going to meet us?"

He nodded. "At 1500 hours. Three o'clock."

She frowned. "Isn't that a long time?"

"Not really. About five hours from now. He needs time for the—sun to melt the snow," he said raggedly. "And we need time to get there. Let's go."

"No." Aimee crouched and unzipped the daypack. She dug in it for the first aid items. "We're not going anywhere until I take care of your arm. You're still bleeding. What did you do?"

He caught her arm. "No."

"Matt, yes! You're about to collapse. You can't go any farther until we stop that bleeding."

"Not here. The tree—"

As if on cue, the branches creaked and scraped across the tin roof.

Of course. The tree. They had to get out of the way, in case it fell. "Come on, then. Let's get away from here."

"Go on," Matt said tightly. "I'll follow."

"Oh, no, you don't. You took care of me when I was hypothermic. It's my turn."

She zipped up the daypack and slung it onto her back, sticking her arms through the straps. "Will it help you to lean on me?"

Matt's mouth turned up in a wry smile. "I already am," he muttered. "More than I should."

After a couple of seconds, he shook his head. "No. Please go on. I'm going to be slower than—than you."

Aimee could tell his voice was getting weaker. *Don't quit on me,* she wanted to say. But that wasn't fair. He'd pushed himself further than she ever would have been able to. He wasn't quitting.

His wounded body was betraying him.

So she headed south for about fifty feet, stopping at a fallen tree trunk that was about the right height for sitting. She brushed snow off and sat to wait for him to catch up.

He walked slowly, doggedly, as if all that was keeping him on his feet was sheer determination. It broke her heart to watch his struggle. It took all her self-control not to run to help him.

Her eyes burned and her throat closed, but she busied herself with unloading the first aid supplies.

When he got to her she looked up, masking her feelings with a smile. "Sit down and let me see your arm."

He didn't even try to argue. He propped the rifle against the tree trunk and slid his parka off his right arm. Then he carefully peeled the sleeve off his left arm, doing his best not to move his arm.

His sweater was soaked with blood. Aimee swallowed against the nausea that rose in her throat. "Sit," she said as evenly as she could.

She took the scissors and cut the sleeves off his arm. "Oh, Matt. What happened? Is that a gunshot wound?"

His back was straight but his eyes were closed. "No," he muttered. "A branch."

"It went—" She twisted his arm slightly so she could see the underside, grimacing when he moaned. "It went all the way through?"

Dear heavens, don't let me hurt him. She knew that was a wasted prayer. She had to clean and wrap his arm. Everything she did was going to hurt him.

"I've got to get your watch off." His hand was swollen and discolored, and the watchband looked unbearably tight. "Please, believe me. I don't want to hurt you, but it's got to come off."

It wasn't easy, and Matt was wheezing in pain by the time she was done, but she got the watch unfastened. She put it on her wrist and buckled it in the last hole.

"Aimee—" he gasped. "Before you—get started, hand me the rifle."

"It's right next to you—" She stopped as understanding dawned. He knew where it was. He just couldn't lean over to get it. Every bit of strength he had was devoted to keeping himself upright. She couldn't imagine what it had cost him to ask her to pick up the rifle and put it in his hand.

She grabbed it and held it so he could get his right arm around it and his finger on the trigger. "Thanks," he breathed.

"I don't have anything to give you for pain," she said as she sat back down and gently touched his arm.

"Just hurry."

As quickly and as gently as she could, she poured alcohol over the top of his arm and caught it with gauze pads underneath. She cleaned both awful, gaping holes as well as she could, doing her best to ignore Matt's harsh breathing and frequent grunts of pain. By the time she was done, sweat was beading on her forehead and Matt had gone quiet.

"I don't know how doctors stand it," she muttered as she squeezed antibiotic ointment onto a clean gauze pad, applied it to the upper wound and did the same with the wound on the underside of his arm. Then she took a roll of gauze and wrapped it around his arm.

"Is that too tight?" she asked.

Matt raised his head a bit and he carefully moved his fingers. "Okay," he said shortly.

She secured the ends of the gauze with adhesive tape.

When she finished, she straightened and examined his face. His skin looked tight and drawn across his cheekbones. His mouth was compressed into a thin line, his nostrils and the corners of his lips were white and pinched. And sweat glistened on his forehead and neck.

"I'm done," she said. "Are you okay?"

"I will be."

She took a last gauze pad and wiped his face and neck, noticing that he was trembling.

"Okay, I've got something for you." She pulled out a self-heating container of hot chocolate. "I figured if I asked, you'd tell me to leave it because it was too heavy. But I think you're going to be glad I have it. I found it in one of the cupboards."

Pressing a button on the bottom of the container, she activated the chemical reaction in the container's sleeve that heated the chocolate drink inside.

"In about ten seconds, this is going to be hot chocolate. You need to drink it."

"We need to go."

"No. You're not going anywhere until you drink this." She waited until the container felt hot in her hands. Then she popped the tab and firmly pressed it into his right hand. "Drink."

"You need—"

"Listen, Matthew Parker. I haven't been out in the snow all night, and I didn't just single-handedly save a helpless infant. And I haven't lost pints and pints of blood. That chocolate's all yours. Besides, I had some already. I'm full."

She didn't miss his sidelong glance. She was lying, and he knew it.

Even though nothing but the nylon shell of her parka was touching the shoulder of his sweater, she felt the shudder that racked him as he swallowed the hot, sweet liquid.

Something shook loose inside her, and tears filled her eyes. Strangely, that had been happening a lot the past few days. She knew what Matt would say—probably what most people would say.

Your child's been kidnapped. It's natural to cry.

But that wasn't true—not for her. She'd decided a long time ago that for her, crying equaled losing control. For her entire adult life she'd prided herself on never crying.

All those times when control had slipped through

her fingers, leaving her feeling helpless and impotent—her parents' deaths, Bill's illness and tragic death, even William's kidnapping—at least she could say she didn't cry.

Ever since she and Matt had joined together to rescue William, she'd begun to look at tears differently. They had more to do with relief and joy and even sadness than with failure on her part.

Right now her tears reflected a poignant concern for Matt and a deep-seated satisfaction that, finally, she was able to give him back a fraction of the help he'd given her. She only hoped the energy in the chocolate drink would be enough to carry him to the rendezvous point. She watched him to make sure he drank every drop.

Matt's first swallow of hot chocolate spread through him like a flame of desire. As soon as it hit his stomach, however, a deep, bone-rattling shudder had racked his body. Partly a result of the hot liquid flowing through his chilled body, warming his insides. But also the clenching response of his empty stomach suddenly being hit with the sugary substance.

Once the initial queasiness passed, he actually felt a little better. The unrelenting pain in his arm was the same, but each throb didn't plaster black-edged stars before his eyes or trigger his gag reflex.

"Why don't you eat an energy bar?" Aimee said. "I've got several."

He squeezed his eyes shut and moved his head a fraction in a negative direction. He knew his gut wouldn't accept the chewy, fiber-rich bar.

"We need to get going." He stood. For a second, the

black-edged stars blinded him again, so he stood still, waiting for them to fade. He wasn't going to get far if the pain in his arm kept up. Just standing jarred it.

"I need you to do something else for me," he said.

Aimee looked up at him. "Anything," she said.

"Do you have any more tape or gauze?"

She looked into the bag. "Both, why? Are you hurt somewhere else?"

"I need you to immobilize my arm against my middle. If it starts bleeding again, I'll probably pass out, so I need to keep it as still as possible."

Aimee cut the left arm of his sweater and his long underwear, all the way up to the neck. Then she wrapped gauze around his wrist and back until his forearm was sealed against his torso. "I don't know how we're going to get your sweater or your undershirt back on."

He shook his head. "Just hand me the parka."

Finally, once he had his parka up over his right shoulder and draped over his left, he cautiously lifted his head, steeling himself against nausea and dizziness.

A flicker of light caught the edge of his vision. He squinted in that direction, but didn't see anything except snowdrifts and fallen trees. Was it his weakness, playing visual tricks on him?

He moved his head back and forth, trying to catch the reflection again. It could have been a piece of ice that caught the sun just right, or a tiny scrap of metal turned up by the snow.

Or it could have been something more ominous, like sunlight glinting off binoculars—or the barrel of a gun.

"Do you need to rest for a little while longer?"

"No," he said, rubbing his temple with his right hand. If someone—Al Hamar—was watching them, he didn't want him to think he'd spotted him.

And he didn't want Aimee to know his suspicion. She wouldn't be able to keep from looking behind them, and that could be fatal. He was still counting on Al Hamar needing him alive. All he had to do was make sure the terrorist couldn't get a clear shot at Aimee.

The only way he could do that was to stay so close to her that Al Hamar couldn't shoot her without running the risk of hitting him.

"I need something else," Matt said.

Aimee looked at him in surprise. "Sure. What do you need?"

"I need to lean on you." He held up Kinnard's rifle. "Hook the rifle over my right shoulder. Then I'm going to put my arm around your shoulders, just to keep me steady."

Aimee bit the inside of her cheek, doing her best not to cry. She saw in his face that he wasn't used to asking for help. "No problem," she said, putting a false brightness into her voice. "I might even get the chance to cop a feel."

She stepped in close enough to him so he could put his arm around her shoulders. "Can I put my arm around your waist without hurting you too much?"

Matt's breathing was fast and short. "I'd be— insulted if you—didn't."

Gingerly, she slid her hand under his parka and wrapped it around his middle, feeling the hard muscles of his back. Even covered by layers of clothes, they felt like long straps of steel.

It terrified her how frail and breakable the human body was. Not many hours ago, his lean, rock-hard body had covered hers, strong, demanding and unbearably sexy as they'd made love.

A thrill tightened her stomach at the memory. It seemed unreal now, like a fantasy, or a dream. It was a moment stolen out of time.

This was reality. Matt injured, needing her support.

Although the arm clutching her shoulders was corded with muscles, he leaned on her heavily, at this moment needing her more than she needed him.

It took a long time to figure out how to walk with Matt so close to her. Finally, once they found a rhythm, it seemed as if he were hardly leaning on her at all.

AIMEE LOOKED at Matt's watch on her wrist. It was two o'clock. She'd been denying the truth for over an hour. But the fact was that Matt was getting weaker—much weaker.

After he'd drunk the chocolate, he'd started out walking strongly, barely even resting his arm on her shoulder.

But the farther they went, the heavier he got. He was losing strength fast. She'd tried to get him to stop and eat something, but he'd refused. She'd forced him to drink a few of sips of water, but the last two times she'd held the bottle for him, he'd shaken his head doggedly and refused.

She was pretty sure her makeshift bandage had stemmed the flow of blood, but not in time. She knew he'd lost too much already. She knew nothing about blood loss or first aid, but it made sense that if he was losing blood he should be drinking water.

"Matt, here. Have some more water."

He shook his head. "Not now," he whispered.

It was the same answer he'd given the last three times she'd asked.

He turned his head to look behind them, as he'd done a number of times. Even though he hadn't said anything, she knew what he was doing. He was worried that someone was behind them, following them.

"I know there's someone following us," she said.

He didn't comment, but she felt a deep breath shudder through him.

"It's the terrorist, isn't it? You told me you found Kinnard dead, so it's got to be Al—Al—?"

"Al Hamar."

"So how do you want to handle him? Just keep ignoring him? It's after one o'clock. We should be getting close to the rendezvous point."

He nodded. "Half a mile—maybe." His voice was nothing more than a raspy whisper.

Half a mile. They'd only come three-fourths of the way? It felt like they'd been walking for hours.

And Matt sounded so weak it made her want to cry. But crying wouldn't accomplish anything. He'd been so strong for her. It was her turn to be strong for him.

"Matt. I'm not taking another step until you drink some water. You of all people should know that if you're losing blood, you should be drinking water." She uncapped the bottle and held it out.

"Drink," she commanded.

He took the plastic bottle, but all he did was fill his mouth. He acted like it was agony to swallow.

"Are you nauseated? Do you want another hot chocolate?" She tried to give him a smile. "It'll do you good."

He shook his head and swallowed the mouthful of water with difficulty. Then he blew out a hard breath, as if the mere act of swallowing had exhausted him.

His face had turned from merely pale to a very scary gray color. And she knew gray-tinged skin was not a good sign.

He wasn't going to make it.

As soon as that thought crossed her mind, her brain screamed in protest.

No. Matt couldn't be dying.

Oh, yes, he could, her rational brain answered her back.

The water bottle fell from his hands.

"Oh, no. That's all we've got!" Aimee let go of Matt and reached for the bottle, which had rolled away. The water represented life to her. If she could get him to drink the water, he'd be okay.

"Aimee!" Matt rasped.

She grabbed the bottle. "We only lost a little bit. It's still half-full."

She turned, holding the bottle up.

But Matt had gone down on one knee. His head was bent and as she watched, the rifle slipped from his shoulder.

"Matt! Oh, I am so sorry." She stood.

He lifted his head. "Get down!" he yelled hoarsely. "Now!"

She dove for the ground, her hands plowing snow in front of her.

Then she heard the gunshot.

Chapter Fourteen

Matt heard the bullet whiz by his ear. His entire body clenched at the sound of the shot.

Ignoring the pain that throbbed through his injured arm, he grabbed the strap of Kinnard's rifle and crawled toward the pile of snow that marked where Aimee had fallen.

"Aimee," he whispered desperately. "Are you okay?"

He saw the top of her head.

"Keep down," he snapped, expecting another shot at any second.

He slithered like a snake across the melting snow until he was close to her. Then he flipped over, so he was facing the shooter.

He was going to have a hell of a time shooting with only one arm, but he could do it if he had to.

Aimee was in danger. He had to take a shot.

Lifting his head up over the top of the snow, he scanned the clearing, but didn't see anything.

"Matt?"

"Don't move." He knew he could outwait the other man. It would be hell to lie in wet snow with the pain in his arm stealing his breath and his fingers going numb again, but he was only minutes from getting Aimee to safety. He wasn't about to give up now.

Clammy sweat stung his eyes and rolled down his neck. His empty stomach cramped, sending nausea crawling up his throat.

There. A flash of sun on metal. He lifted the rifle with his right hand and looked through the scope, but he couldn't focus.

His eyes were blurry. He lowered the rifle and bent his head to wipe his eyes on his sleeve, but his sleeve was wet.

"Here," Aimee said. From somewhere, she pulled a dry piece of cloth and handed it to him.

He wiped his eyes and face. She took the cloth back. "Can I do something to help you hold the rifle? I could lie down and you could prop it on my back."

Matt barely heard her. Something else had grabbed his attention. He cocked his head and listened. He wasn't sure if he could trust his ears. He'd already found out he couldn't completely trust his eyes.

He rolled onto his right shoulder and looked up. He had heard the rhythmic whup-whup of helicopter blades.

Aimee followed his gaze. She gasped. "Matt! Is it Deke?"

Without waiting for him to answer, she waved her arms. "He's here! Deke!" she cried.

"Aimee, don't!" His left arm jerked, an instinctive move to try and grab her. He couldn't stop an involuntary cry. He sucked in a breath.

"He sees us."

Just as she pulled her arms down, another shot rang out.

"Ow!" she cried, grabbing her hand.

Matt pushed himself up onto his right elbow. "Aimee! Are you hit?"

She looked at her hand. "I felt something hot—but I don't see anything."

"Give me your hand."

He examined it closely. There was a tiny red scrape along the flesh of her palm below her little finger. "Looks like the bullet barely missed you."

He closed his eyes for a second, willing away the dizziness and blurred vision. Then he glared at her. "Could you please stay still, and do what I tell you?"

She bit her lip and her cheeks turned pink. "Yes, sir," she whispered.

"Bastard's desperate. He knows once Deke lands he's got no chance to kill you or capture me." He raised his head again, scanning the area for the shooter. "We've got to stay down until Deke lands," he told Aimee. "If Al Hamar starts shooting at the helicopter, Deke will have to abort."

"Abort?"

Matt nodded grimly. "We can't afford to lose the helicopter, or Deke. But don't worry. He's got a high-powered rifle on board. Maybe even a machine gun. He'll be back, loaded for bear."

She nodded, but her eyes were wide with fear.

"Our job is to stay down until he can put down. If I can, I'm going to take out Al Hamar when he tries to shoot the helicopter again. I'd like to take the SOB alive, but that may not be possible. The most important thing is to get you out of here."

"No," she snapped. "The most important thing is to

get *you* on that helicopter and to a hospital. I'll take my chances."

Matt felt his chapped, cracked lips widen in a smile. It hurt but he didn't care. He raised his brows. "You'll take your chances…"

Her cheeks got pinker, but she lifted her chin. "That's right. In fact, why don't you give me that rifle and I'll take care of Al Hamar, or whatever his name is."

The terrorist was shooting again, this time at the helicopter. Over the sound of the rotors, Matt heard the zing of a bullet ricocheting off metal.

Deke took the bird up a few dozen feet, but he didn't turn away.

Matt squinted up at him. "Come on, Cunningham. That's just stupid."

"What? What's the matter?"

"Deke's drawing his fire." Matt swiped his forehead on the sleeve of his parka again and flipped over onto his stomach, suppressing a groan.

"Why?"

Matt swallowed the bile that was threatening to erupt from his throat. He felt like he was about to puke his guts up. The good news was that his arm had quit hurting. It was just numb.

Or was that the bad news?

Pushing away those thoughts, he lifted the rifle and sighted through the scope. "He knows our terrorist friend's got to come out from his cover to get a shot at him. He's drawing him out so I can shoot him." He blew out a harsh breath. "I hope I can."

Aimee scooted over closer to him.

"I told you—"

"Matt, lean on me. Use me to brace the gun."

Matt's right arm was shaking with fatigue and weakness from loss of blood. He shook his head. "I can't even figure out what you're talking about."

"Here. Move over." She crawled around until her body was perpendicular to his. "Now let me lie down in front of you and you can brace the gun on my back. Won't that work?"

He didn't want to tell her that most of what she'd just said sounded like gibberish to his buzzing ears. He just watched as she lay flat on her stomach in front of him. "Now, can you brace the barrel of the rifle on me?"

Slowly, his brain processed her words. "Maybe so," he whispered. "I can try."

"Listen," Aimee said. "Deke's coming lower. Al Hamar will probably shoot at him." She took a long breath. "Get ready."

Matt set the barrel of the rifle across her shoulders and pushed himself forward until he could see through the scope. "Aimee?"

"Yeah?"

He blinked sweat out of his eyes, and swept the scope back and forth, looking for the terrorist. "I love you."

Her body stiffened, making the scope wobble. "Hey. Stay still. I almost had him."

"Are you okay?" she asked, a worried tone in her voice. "You sound like you've been drinking."

"Hold still." He concentrated all the energy he had left in him on watching through the scope. Then he saw him. Al Hamar. He'd slipped out from behind a tree to get a shot at Deke. He'd braced himself and was aiming at the helicopter that loomed over their heads.

"Don't move," Matt whispered. "I've got him." His vision wavered, but hell, it was a short shot. And the guy was presenting a perfect target, the way he stood with his feet apart. It was a sucker shot.

Slowly, carefully, Matt squeezed the trigger. He saw the man jerk, saw blood blossom on the leg of his pants. As he watched, the terrorist dropped to his knees.

Then the man turned the rifle on Matt. For an instant they were scope to scope, then Al Hamar shifted his barrel downward. He was going to shoot Aimee.

Matt pulled the trigger again and again and again.

The last thing he remembered was a burst of bright stars before his eyes.

SUNDAY 2000 HOURS

THE CLEAN WHITE SHEETS and pillow felt like heaven to Aimee's exhausted muscles and chapped skin. Even the cotton hospital gown couldn't have felt better if it were the finest silk.

But what felt better than all that, even better than the warm bathwater or the delicious hot soup they'd given her, was the tiny bundle that was nestled into the crook of her arm.

She looked down at William. He was asleep. He'd seemed singularly unconcerned that she'd been gone. As soon as she'd stopped kissing him all over his face and touching every tiny perfect finger and toe, he'd fallen right to sleep.

"Must be nice," she murmured drowsily, "to be so sure that everything's fine in your world." She chuckled softly. "Know what, William? I think they gave me something to make me sleepy." She reached for the cup of water on the bedside table and took a small sip, letting the cool wetness slide down her throat. "I'm just going to take a little nap while you're sleeping. Then when I wake up, we'll go find Matt."

Matt. Her heart gave a slight jump. Deke had told her he was going to be fine. Hadn't he? Her eyes drifted closed.

Or had she dreamed it?

She didn't remember much after Deke got them into the helicopter. Just his deep, reassuring voice, saying everything was going to be all right.

But what else was he going to say in that situation? *Sorry, guys, looks like you're not going to make it?*

Then he'd put the helicopter down on the roof of the hospital and all kinds of mayhem had broken out. Men and women dressed in blue with rolling tables had rushed out into the wind and grabbed Matt.

Aimee remembered trying to see where they took him, but more people ran out and grabbed her. Somebody leaned over her and said something, and that was all she remembered until she woke up while a nurse's aide was bathing her.

Nurse. The nurses could tell her about Matt. She reached for the call button. Her movement disturbed William and he whimpered.

"Sorry, baby. I'm just going to call the nurse." But her arm was tired, and her eyelids were heavy. "In a minute," she whispered and tucked her arm closer around her baby.

THEY WERE BACK. Parker and Aimee Vick. According to a brief message from Irina, Parker was in surgery and expected to be okay, Aimee was fine, and she and her child had been reunited.

He couldn't deny that he was relieved that the child hadn't been harmed.

But how the hell had Parker managed to outsmart Kinnard at every turn? Kinnard knew these hills and conditions better than anyone he'd ever known. Parker was supposed to be a weather specialist and something of a survival expert, but Kinnard had at least three inches and fifty pounds on him, plus all the time Parker had been overseas in the military, Kinnard had been roaming the mountains, learning how to survive. Having been a Marine, he already knew how to fight.

He had to find out what had happened out there.

His cell phone rang. He glanced at the display. It was Irina's administrative assistant, Pam Jamieson.

"There's a briefing in the conference room in twenty," she said, all business as usual.

"Got it," he responded.

Good. He'd have information to pass on tonight. He glanced at his watch. He had just enough time to check on the next phase of the plan. With any luck, by this time tomorrow, Deke Cunningham would no longer be protected by the security surrounding Castle Ranch.

MATT JERKED. The terrorist! He was shooting at Aimee! Matt tried to pull the trigger, but he couldn't. Something was wrong with his hand.

He opened his eyes. All he saw was blue and white. Blue walls, low blue light. White sheets.

Sheets?

He looked down at himself. He was covered up to his chest by a white sheet. His left arm was wrapped up like a mummy and his right arm was strapped down, with tubes running in several different directions.

What the hell? He felt drugged. The way he'd felt years ago when he'd woken up from an emergency appendectomy. His eyes burned and his mouth was dry, but not as dry as it had been. His arm hurt, but not as badly as it had before.

Before what?

Closing his eyes, he tried to wipe his mind free of all the confusing and disturbing images that were clicking through it like a slide show gone out of control.

—Aimee, lying so close to the spreading pool of gasoline.

—Kinnard pointing that assault rifle at her.

—His own arm impaled by a sharp piece of wood.

—Kinnard's girl jerking as the bullet hit her head.

—Deke hauling up the basket carrying its precious cargo.

Matt growled and opened his eyes. Closing them had only sped up the slide show. He stared at the ceiling, counting off the pictures as they flashed across his inner vision, trying to pick out the latest ones and shuffle them into some sort of order.

He remembered Aimee waving at Deke, and the horrifying sight of the red dot wavering on the front of her parka.

He remembered her lying down in front of him so he could use her as a prop for the rifle barrel. He remembered pulling the trigger again and again and again.

But for the life of him he couldn't remember anything after that. What a weakling he was. Some rescuer he was. It was pretty bad when the rescuer himself had to be rescued.

It was a good thing Deke was there, because if it had been left up to him, Aimee would probably be dead now.

Aimee. He had to find her—check on her. He looked around for the nurse call button, and discovered that someone had had the foresight to put it next to his right hand. With more effort than he'd have thought he'd need, he lifted his hand enough to get his finger on the button and pressed it.

"—help you?"

"Get me a nurse now!" What he heard in his ears was nothing like what he'd intended. He'd barked a command, but a raspy whisper was all that had come out of his mouth. Plus the very act of punching the button and speaking had started his heart hammering and his head pounding.

He closed his eyes and pretended that the dampness that leaked out from under his lids wasn't tears.

"Mr. Parker, are you all right?"

He turned his head enough to see the pretty young woman dressed in some kind of smock with dogs and cats on it.

"Get me unhooked from all this stuff. I've got to check on Aimee."

The young woman smiled as she stepped over to the bed and patted his hand. "I'm glad to see you're awake and feeling better, but you're not going to be able to get up for a while. You've only been out of the recovery room for an hour or so."

"Recovery room?"

"The surgery on your arm." She punched some buttons

on the monitor that was beeping behind his head, and checked the bag of fluid that hung on a pole beside him.

"Everything looks good. You have some visitors who have been waiting for you to wake up. They're down in the coffee shop. I'll call them, and in a few minutes, I'll bring you a sleeping pill."

"Visitors? Is it Aimee?"

"Aimee? The young woman who was brought in with you? No." She pulled off gloves he hadn't noticed she had on and pumped a bit of antiseptic gel on her hands from a dispenser hanging on the wall.

"Wait a minute. Where am I?"

She pointed at a whiteboard, hanging on the wall directly across from his bed, where the name of the hospital, the date and the names of his nurses and aides were written. "You're in Crook County Hospital. Today is Sunday and my name is Jean. I'll be back soon."

Matt studied the tubes and needles that were sticking out of his right hand, trying to decide how much it would hurt to pull them out. He wanted to look more closely at them but for some reason he found it very hard to lift his arm. So he turned his attention to his other arm. He still had his hand. It was sticking out from the huge roll of bandages. It looked swollen and discolored, but at least it was there.

Before he had a chance to wonder what the surgeons had done to it, the room door opened and Irina Castle came in, followed by Brock O'Neill and FBI Special Agent Schiff.

"Matt! Oh my goodness, you look awful!" She laughed self-consciously as she stepped around to the far side of the bed and patted his hand. "I mean, you look wonderful, given all that you've been through. How are you feeling?"

Brock nodded and scowled as if he were irritated to see Matt alive. But that was his usual expression, so Matt merely nodded back.

"Where's Aimee?" he asked Irina.

"She and William are doing fine. Aimee's been admitted overnight, but they should be able to go home tomorrow." Irina looked at Schiff.

He stepped forward. "Sorry, but we need to talk to you."

Matt ignored him. "Irina, Aimee can't go home by herself. She's been through too much. Can you do something? I don't think it's a good idea for her to have to depend on Margo."

"Don't worry. We're going to take good care of her." She picked up the cup of water and held the straw to his lips. He took a couple of swallows and coughed.

"Margo Vick won't be going anywhere near Aimee," Schiff said. "Not anytime soon. I can promise you that."

"What are you talking about?"

"Once we found out that the baby was being held at the Vicks' hunting cabin, we got a warrant for Mrs. Vick's financial and telephone records, and her home. We found that a million dollars had been liquidated within the past week. Mrs. Vick and her accountant claim to know nothing about it. There were also two calls to Margo Vick's home telephone from a survivalist group of which Kinnard is a member."

"*Was* a member," Matt said.

Schiff's eyebrows rose.

"Kinnard's dead. I'll give you a statement, and I can

pinpoint the location of the body within a few yards."
Matt didn't mention Shellie. He'd give a formal, complete statement later.

The FBI special agent pulled a PDA from his pocket and made a quick note, then continued. "The telephone calls from the survivalist group were short, less than a minute. Mrs. Vick stated that she received a couple of calls in the past week, and she was asked to hold. She said she held for a short while, and then hung up."

Matt cut his eyes over to the FBI special agent. "It's possible she was framed."

"I know. It's beginning to look that way."

That surprised Matt. He lifted his head and immediately regretted it. The movement hurt his arm and he felt queasy. "What do you mean?" he asked softly.

"We picked up the body of the second man who was following you. Cunningham gave us the coordinates. He was carrying a cell phone, with a message from an unidentified number. The message was in Arabic. We got it translated. Basically, it said—" Schiff looked back at his PDA "—KILL KIDNAPPERS. NO SURVIVORS TO ID US."

Matt's pulse jumped. "The kidnapper *was* hired by Novus."

"Novus?" Schiff frowned. "The terrorist Novus?" He turned to glare at Irina.

When he did, Brock took a step closer to her.

"I figured the dead guy might be somehow involved with your search for your husband, but *Novus Ordo?*"

Irina gazed at him evenly.

"Well, that explains a lot. Not everything, but a lot. We had the voice of the caller who set up the ransom drop analyzed. There were certain inflections and idiomatic inconsistencies that indicated that English may not have been his first language."

"May not?" Irina repeated.

Schiff nodded. "The results were inconclusive. My expert said it was possible that the caller was trying to alter his phrasing to make us think he might not be American."

Matt closed his eyes and sighed. "So we can't prove whether the whole thing was engineered by Novus or not."

"It would help if all the people involved in the kidnapping weren't dead. Couldn't you have left one of them alive?"

"Agent Schiff," Irina broke in. "Matt needs to sleep. He's still under the effects of the anesthesia from his surgery."

Schiff sent her a sharp glance. "Fine. I'll get his statement tomorrow, when he's feeling better. Mrs. Castle, may I speak to you after we're done here?"

She put her hand on Matt's forehead and brushed his hair back. "We'll see."

"Irina, what about—what about the sabotage?" Matt whispered.

Irina leaned over. "We'll talk about that later," she said softly.

Just then the nurse came in. "It's time for Mr. Parker's medication."

Irina kissed him on the forehead. "Don't worry about Aimee," she whispered. "I'll see you tomorrow."

Brock hadn't said a word the entire time. In fact, he'd hardly moved, except when he'd intercepted Schiff. He'd just listened intently to everything that was said.

As Irina and Schiff left the room, Brock met Matt's gaze and nodded, the scowl still on his face.

The nurse injected something into the IV tubing that ran from the bag of fluid down into his hand. "There you go, Mr. Parker." She peeled off her exam gloves, then turned and looked at him.

"Who was that man?" she asked, her eyes wide and her cheeks flushed.

"The guy in the suit?"

"No. The one with the eye patch. The dangerous-looking one. Who was he?"

Matt's eyelids were getting heavy. "You mean Brock O'Neill?" he muttered. "That's a real good question. I'm not sure any of us know who he is." He peered at her. "You want me to introduce you?"

She laughed and shook her head. "Oh, no. I was married to a dangerous man once. I'll never make that mistake again. You get some sleep and I'll be back later to check your vital signs."

MONDAY 1100 HOURS

THE DOOR TO MATT'S hospital room was closed. It had taken Aimee much longer than she'd anticipated to be discharged, although the doctor had promised her yesterday that he was only admitting her overnight for observation. The nurses on her floor had brought her a set of scrubs to wear and had outfitted William with clothes from the pediatric floor.

But now, finally, she was here. She was supposed to be waiting downstairs for a taxi that the floor clerk had called, and she felt slightly guilty for leaving the driver sitting there, but she had to see Matt.

She shifted William's baby seat to her left hand and started to knock. But she hesitated. What if he were asleep? Or being given a bath? Or what if he didn't want to see her?

She took a deep breath. No matter what he wanted, she *was* going to see him, if only for a few minutes. She wasn't about to leave the hospital without making sure he was okay.

"If he's asleep, we'll go," she whispered to William. Instead of knocking, she gently pushed the door open.

The room was dark. The curtains were closed. The only light came from the weak, recessed fixture above the bed. He was asleep.

She knew she should turn around and leave, but she couldn't take her eyes off him. She'd been so afraid he wouldn't make it. They'd taken him away so fast once the helicopter had landed.

She moved carefully over to the bed, hoping that William would stay quiet. The shadows cast by the dim light emphasized the pain lines etched between his brows and around his mouth.

His hair was a little bit tousled, enough that she wanted to reach out and brush it back from his forehead. And his mouth was as straight and grim as it had been the last time she'd seen him, right before the emergency doctors had taken him off the helicopter and rolled him away.

"I'm so sorry," she mouthed, not really sure why she was apologizing. Mostly that he'd been hurt so badly for trying to help her, she supposed.

"You've got nothing to be sorry for," he whispered.

She jumped, jostling the baby seat. William made a tiny whimper of protest, but Aimee couldn't take her eyes off Matt.

He opened his eyes, those deep, dark eyes, and looked at her.

"Matt," she breathed, her pulse hammering in her throat. "You're—okay?"

His mouth curved up slightly. "Depends on what you mean by *okay*. I'm here, and essentially in one piece." He lifted his right hand, which was attached to what looked like a tangle of tubing, and pressed a button on the bed. The head of the bed raised up.

He winced slightly, and Aimee's gaze went to his left arm, which was covered by a fat bandage. "What—what did they say about your arm?"

His long, dark lashes swept downward. "The doctor came in earlier. He said all I needed to know was that they cleaned the wound, sewed some muscles and tendons back together, and stitched it all up." He looked down at the bandage. "He said it wouldn't be pretty, but with a little luck and a lot of physical therapy, it would probably work okay, thanks to whoever cleaned and bandaged it."

Aimee took a long breath. "I'm so glad."

"Me, too, although I have a feeling he really meant a *lot* of luck." He raised his gaze to hers. "How are you? You look good."

"I'm good," she said, nodding. "I'm fine. I brought someone to see you."

"William—?" Matt's voice broke, and Aimee's heart felt like it was cracking in two.

She smiled. "He wants to say thank you." She swallowed the lump that had risen in her throat.

"Let me see him."

She set the baby seat down and took William into her arms. "Can I sit down?" She nodded toward the side of his bed.

"Sure. Bring him over here."

She bounced the baby in her arms as she walked around and sat gingerly on the edge of the bed. She propped William on her lap.

Matt lifted his right hand, then checked his gesture. "Think the tubes will scare him?"

As if in answer, William cooed and waved his arms.

"I don't think anything about you could possibly scare him. He's happy to see you."

"Yeah?"

"William? You know who this is? Remember Matt? He's your godfather. He saved you."

"Aimee, don't—" Matt's hand fell back to the bed.

"Don't what? Tell my son the truth? You did save him. You saved him and me."

Matt leaned his head back and closed his eyes. "If you're going to tell him the truth, tell him the whole truth. Tell him what happened to his father. Tell him that I didn't have the sense or the courage to refuse to take Bill skydiving. I didn't have the good sense to make him take some practice runs or do a buddy-dive."

"Bill had skydived before. His carelessness wasn't your responsibility."

Matt blinked. "Why have you suddenly changed your mind?"

"Changed my mind? What are you talking about?"

"Are you feeling sorry for me? Is that it? What happened to blaming me for letting him die?"

"I never blamed you."

"Hah." He squeezed his eyes shut and shook his head. "I saw how you looked at me when I brought his—when I brought him home."

"Matt, I can't remember what I did or said or even thought that night. What I do remember is what Bill always told me. 'You can count on Matt.' He said that the day before you and he left on your trip. 'Matt's safe as houses.'"

Matt lifted his head and looked at her. "I don't know why he thought that."

"I do, now."

He stared at her, his dark eyes glittering with unshed tears.

"It took me a while to understand what he meant. He knew you, maybe better than anyone. He knew you'd die, if by dying you could save an innocent life."

He shrugged and winced. "For some reason, Bill always believed in me."

William was getting restless. He began to fret. "I guess I'd better put this little guy back in his seat."

"Can I—?"

Aimee knew what Matt was trying to ask. She held William close enough that Matt could press a kiss to his fat little cheek. "Hey there, William," he whispered. "Are you glad to see your mom?"

She turned to fasten William back into his seat.

"Aimee?" She didn't look up. She was busy blinking away the tears that she couldn't stop. Seeing Matt kissing her little boy had shattered the last fragile pieces of her heart.

"Aimee—"

She lifted her head without really looking at him. "I'm listening. I just need to get William Matthew settled."

"Could you—maybe one day—give me a chance?"

She froze for an instant, wondering if she'd heard what she thought she had. Then she tested the last strap, to be sure William was safe in his seat.

Slowly, she raised her gaze to his. "Give you a chance?"

The muscles of his jaw worked. "I—" He swallowed. "I love you."

She gasped softly. "You said that before. I thought you were hallucinating."

He shook his head. "I wasn't hallucinating." Then his gaze wavered.

She'd seen him face killer snowstorms, assault rifles, gasoline fires, a horrible injury, but this was the first time she'd seen him nearly paralyzed with fear.

Her mouth stretched into a grin, even as fat tears slipped from her eyes and plopped onto her hands. "I am—so glad," she said, her voice shaking with sobs. "Because I wasn't sure how I was going to—tell you that I fell in—love with you the minute you bullied me into letting you go to the ransom drop with me."

"You did?" he said, his brows shooting up.

"Well, it didn't hurt that you made the supreme sacrifice of warming me with your own naked body."

"Anytime," he said, smiling at her.

"Promise?"

"You—" He paused. "You're okay with me being William's stepfather? I mean—are you saying you'll—you know?"

"I have something to tell you. When Bill found out he had cancer, he made me promise him something."

"Yeah? What?" Matt still looked scared.

"He made me promise that when I was ready, I'd think about you first."

She'd done pretty well so far, but remembering Bill's words and thinking about how prophetic they were, she looked at the man she knew would keep her and her son safe. Love and desire welled up inside her, and pushed away the last bits of the rigid control she'd always clung to like a lifeline. For the first time in her life, she broke down and sobbed.

Matt lifted his hand. "Aimee, are you okay?"

"Sure." She sniffed.

"You're crying."

"I know," she wailed.

Matt's mouth curved into a smile. "Does that mean this qualifies as a special occasion?"

She leaned over and kissed him on the mouth as tears streamed down her face. "I think it qualifies as the first in a lifetime of special occasions."

HARLEQUIN
60 YEARS
of pure reading pleasure

We'll be spotlighting a different series
every month throughout 2009
to celebrate our 60ᵗʰ anniversary.

Look for Silhouette® Nocturne™ in October!

Travel through time to experience tales
that reach the boundaries of life and death.
Bestselling authors Lindsay McKenna, Cindy
Dees, P.C. Cast and Merline Lovelace join
together in a brand-new, four-book
Time Raiders miniseries.

TIME RAIDERS

August—*The Seeker*
by *USA TODAY* bestselling author Lindsay McKenna

September—*The Slayer* by Cindy Dees

October—*The Avenger*
by *New York Times* bestselling author and
coauthor of the House of Night novels P.C. Cast

November—*The Protector*
by *USA TODAY* bestselling author Merline Lovelace

Available wherever books are sold.

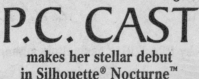

Silhouette®

Romantic
SUSPENSE

Sparked by Danger,
Fueled by Passion.

The Agent's Secret Baby

by *USA TODAY* bestselling author

Marie Ferrarella

TOP SECRET DELIVERIES

Dr. Eve Walters suddenly finds herself pregnant
after a regrettable one-night stand and turns to an
online chat room for support. She eventually learns
the true identity of her one-night stand: a DEA agent
with a deadly secret. Adam Serrano does not want
this baby or a relationship, but can fear for Eve's
and the baby's lives convince him that this is what
he has been searching for after all?

Available October wherever books are sold.

**Look for upcoming titles in
the TOP SECRET DELIVERIES miniseries**

The Cowboy's Secret Twins by Carla Cassidy—November
The Soldier's Secret Daughter by Cindy Dees—December

Visit Silhouette Books at www.eHarlequin.com

SRS27650

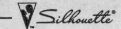

SPECIAL EDITION

FROM *NEW YORK TIMES*
BESTSELLING AUTHOR

SUSAN MALLERY

DESERT
ROGUES

THE SHEIK AND THE BOUGHT BRIDE

Victoria McCallan works in Prince Kateb's palace.
When Victoria's gambling father is caught cheating
at cards with the prince, Victoria saves her father from
going to jail by being Kateb's mistress for six months.
But the darkly handsome desert sheik isn't as harsh as
Victoria thinks he is, and Kateb finds himself attracted to
his new mistress. But Kateb has already loved and lost
once—is he willing to give love another try?

Available in October wherever books are sold.

SSE65481

REQUEST YOUR FREE BOOKS!

2 FREE NOVELS PLUS 2 FREE GIFTS!

HARLEQUIN®
INTRIGUE®

Breathtaking Romantic Suspense

You're invited to join our Tell Harlequin Reader Panel!

By joining our new reader panel you will:

- Receive Harlequin® books—they are FREE and yours to keep with no obligation to purchase anything!
- Participate in fun online surveys
- Exchange opinions and ideas with women just like you
- Have a say in our new book ideas and help us publish the best in women's fiction

In addition, you will have a chance to win great prizes and receive special gifts! See Web site for details. Some conditions apply. Space is limited.

To join, visit us at
www.TellHarlequin.com.

HARLEQUIN®

INTRIGUE®

COMING NEXT MONTH

Available October 13, 2009

#1161 ONE HOT FORTY-FIVE by B.J. Daniels
Whitehorse, Montana: The Corbetts
He's a practicing lawyer with a cowboy streak, and his wild side has been on hold…until he senses the danger that threatens the one woman who sees his true self.

#1162 THE SHARPSHOOTER'S SECRET SON
by Mallory Kane
Black Hills Brotherhood
The air force taught him honor and responsibility, but it was his ex-wife who taught him to love. When she's kidnapped by a group of terrorists trying to bait him, he makes it his mission to rescue her and rekindle the past they once shared.

#1163 CHRISTMAS GUARDIAN by Delores Fossen
Texas Paternity
Despite his dark past, the millionaire security agent falls for the helpless infant left on his doorstep. But when the baby's mother returns—with killers following close behind—he vows to protect his son and the woman who has captured his heart.

#1164 INTERNAL AFFAIRS by Jessica Andersen
Bear Claw Creek Crime Lab
She is shocked when her ex-lover, an internal affairs investigator, returns from the dead. Injured and unable to remember who he is, all he knows is there is an urgent mission he must complete.

#1165 COLORADO ABDUCTION by Cassie Miles
Christmas at the Carlisles
When her ranch becomes a target for sabotage just weeks before Christmas, the FBI send one of their most domineering and stubborn agents to ferret out the truth. And as the attacks escalate, so does the passion.

#1166 AGENT DADDY by Alice Sharpe
To take care of his orphaned niece and nephew, the FBI agent resigns from his dangerous job. But when his past follows him to the ranch, he fights for the new life—and love—he's just found.

HICNMBPA0909